HOPEBREAKER

BOOKS BY DEAN F. WILSON

THE CHILDREN OF TELM

Book One: The Call of Agon
Book Two: The Road to Rebirth
Book Three: The Chains of War

THE GREAT IRON WAR

Hopebreaker

THE GREAT IRON WAR - BOOK ONE

HOPEBREAKER

DEAN F. WILSON

Cover illustration by Duy Phan

First Edition 2014

ISBN 978-1-909356-08-5

Published by Dioscuri Press
Dublin, Ireland

www.dioscuripress.com
enquiries@dioscuripress.com

SF
Pbk

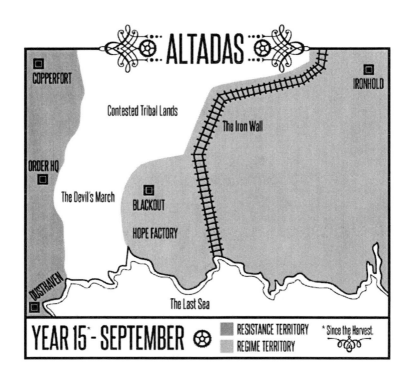

CONTENTS

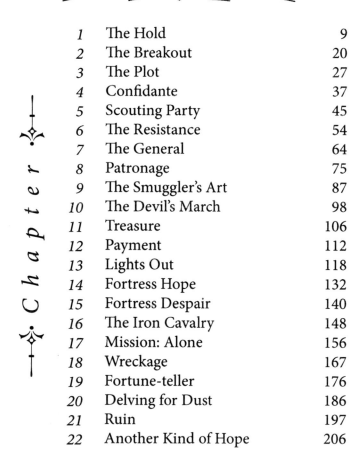

Chapter One

THE HOLD

The walls crashed down and the soldiers stormed in, replacing bricks with leather boots and stones with clenched fists. The dissonance died down, but the dust hung for endless moments, dimming the light and stinging the eyes. Yet Jacob did not need to see; he knew why they were here, what they had come for.

A figure, tall and broad, stepped into view, his hair and uniform as black as the long shadow he cast across the room. His fists were not clasped, but the anger was still there, pouring out of the cracks and crevices of his crooked face. Everyone could recognise him, even in darkness—*especially* in darkness. Everyone knew his name. *Domas.* Yet not everyone knew what he was.

"You are accused of smuggling amulets," Domas said. He paced to and fro restlessly, until the very floor began to recognise him. The light from the oil lamp flickered on his face, creating and killing lots of little shadows. Those shadows made him look inhuman, but under any other light he looked like everybody else. Jacob remembered when he was first told about them by his father. *They are like you and I. They walk among us.*

"What evidence do you have?" Jacob asked, hoping they would not search the bookcase, hoping they would not scour his soul.

Domas drew close, seizing Jacob by the collar. "I don't *need* evidence."

Jacob parried Domas' glower with his own. He felt like responding, like snapping or biting, even though he knew it would not help. It would make him feel better for the briefest of moments, and then, as the soldiers responded with their fists, it would make him feel much worse. The words of his father haunted him like a demon. *In time they will replace us.*

"Take him to the Hold," Domas barked to one of his commanders. He turned to leave, but halted as something caught his eye. "Open your hand," he ordered.

"It's a bit late to shake it."

"Open your hand," Domas repeated. He did not need to give a warning. His tone gave enough.

Jacob offered his left hand, which was empty.

"A clown as well as a smuggler," Domas said. "Your other hand."

Jacob reluctantly loosened his grip on the tiny bag of coils he was holding, his all too meagre payment for smuggling an amulet into the city. Domas snatched it from his grasp.

"You won't be needing this," he said. "In the Hold, the rent is free."

The soldiers seized Jacob and pulled him outside, where a mechanised wagon waited, one of the many vehicles the Regime used to transport its forces—and its prisoners.

In moments Jacob was hauled up and hurled into the back of the warwagon, where he banged his head against the iron walls. He heard the cogs and pistons start up, and he heard the roar of the furnace and the rhythm of the wheels.

The smell of coal and smoke filled his nostrils and seeped into his lungs, until finally he faded off into a halfway place between the waking world and dreams, where he imagined what things might have been like if the demons had not come here, if the Regime had not gained power.

Steel screeched and iron clanged, but the noise was deafened by a louder clunk as Jacob's body hit the cold, stone ground. It hurt almost as much as being slammed into the wagon by the Regime's guards. The footsteps faded and the clangs grew distant, leaving him alone in his cell.

But he was not alone. Jacob barely had time to nurse his wounds before he heard a voice from the shadows in the corner.

"It's about time," it said. The voice was weak and broken. If it belonged to a body, that body must have been weak and broken too.

"Who's there?" Jacob asked as he sat up. He peered into the darkness, where he saw a frail figure, so thin it barely cast a shadow of its own.

"My name's Whistler," the voice said, and the figure leaned forward into the light cast from the oil lamp in the hallway. He looked very young, and very fragile. He collapsed back into the shadow with a sigh.

"How long have you been in here?" Jacob asked. He thought he could make out markings on the wall.

"A month, maybe two," Whistler said. "I stopped keeping count."

"Why haven't they killed you yet?"

"Maybe they can't see me here in the corner," Whistler said with a laugh interrupted by a chesty cough. "I guess they … I guess they prefer torture."

The word brought back memory to Jacob's muscles, which began to throb and sting and ache, little tortures of their own. A shiver slithered up his spine at the grim realisation that he too might face the Iron Chambers.

"You look too young to be a smuggler," Jacob said. "How old are you?"

"Fourteen," Whistler said. "Old enough to die."

"You haven't died yet."

Jacob imagined Whistler was smiling in the darkness. "Give it another year then."

"So what are you then if you're not a smuggler?"

"Have you heard of the Order?"

The mention of the Order brought a flicker of anger into Jacob's soul. They were the reason he was here. They made the amulets. They hired him to get them out to the public. He was just the messenger, soon to be shot.

"So you're one of *them*," Jacob said at last, attempting to conceal his scorn.

"You say that like I'm a demon," Whistler responded. "Can't blame you though. I know how the Order sees you guys. You're just hired to deliver our work. The Order doesn't care if you live or die, and no one will come to rescue you if you get caught."

"And what about you?" Jacob quizzed. "Is someone going to rescue you?"

There was a sharp silence, as if the question struck too deep. Eventually Whistler responded, his voice even weaker than before. "They're coming. They're supposed to come. They'll be here."

You don't sound too sure of that, Jacob thought. *I wouldn't be either.*

They simmered in the silence for a while, until Whistler broke it with his hoarse voice. "How did you get caught?"

Jacob sighed. "A deal gone sour. I asked too much for an amulet, so the woman just turned me in, ratted me out. She claims she was an informer all along, but I don't buy it. I think she just wasn't willing to pay the market price for proper protection."

The thought of it still angered Jacob. He was risking his life so that women could avoid giving birth to demon spawn. He should have been seen as a hero, and paid like a hero. Instead he would rot away in the Hold, and soon be forgotten—as if he had never been born.

"What were you charging?" Whistler asked.

"A hundred coils."

"Hell," Whistler said.

Jacob smirked. "Just where I've been condemned to."

"And you thought she'd really pay that much?"

"I thought I had the bargaining power," Jacob replied. "She wanted an amulet. I wanted more coils. She'll probably spend more trying to find another smuggler anyway."

"Finding a real one, yeah. The Regime has infiltrators everywhere."

"Yes, she'll probably regret not paying," Jacob said mournfully, knowing that he regretted it much more than she ever would. "The Regime will probably track her down one day."

"Let's hope not. We're already losing too many people. *Real* people," Whistler said, running his bony fingers through his bedraggled hair. "Where's the Pure when you need them, eh?"

"Still in the mythology books, kid, still being read as children's bedtime stories."

"If there were any real children," Whistler said. He clawed at the back of his neck and looked back and forth around the room, as if there might be someone watching them. Then he leaned closer to Jacob and whispered, "You know, I'm one of the Last."

Jacob was not surprised. Even if Whistler had not revealed his age, he looked and sounded far too young to have been born before the Harvest, the time when the Regime came into power and began to control all births. That was fifteen years ago. Fifteen years of war. There were not many born since then, and they were known as the Last, but there were frequent rumours about the Pure being able to give real birth, rumours that Jacob did not believe. He was not sure if he wanted to believe. If nothing else, it would put him out of a job.

Jacob did not know how to respond to Whistler's revelation. "You get the last turn then," he said. "How did you get caught?"

"I was a bit loose-lipped," Whistler said at last, but the words did not come easy. He gulped harshly and continued, "I thought I had made a friend. Daniel, someone in the Order. I was supposed to report infiltrators like him, but I wanted a friend so badly I got careless. I blabbed to him about all kinds of things, probably put the Order in big danger. Guess I deserve to be here."

"No one deserves to be here, Whistler," Jacob said, though he might have made an exception for the Iron Emperor. "No one deserves to be tortured or killed by a corrupt government that clings to power by exerting it constantly on its people."

"You sound like Taberah," Whistler said wistfully.

"Who's that?"

"The head of the Order." Whistler paused and slapped his head. "See, I'm doing it again. They don't need to torture me for information. They just need to sit me down and get me yapping."

"I won't tell them any of this," Jacob said. "And I probably won't see the outside world again, so I guess I won't be telling anyone else either."

"Somehow I trust you," Whistler said. "I don't know why, but I do. Then again, I thought I trusted Daniel too."

"He'll pay for his betrayal, I'm sure," Jacob said, confident that he would. The Order was often as merciless as the Regime itself. It had to be. It was the only way to live in this world.

Whistler bowed his head and sighed gravely. "Part of me doesn't want him to. I don't hate them. The Regime, I mean. I know why others do, but I don't want to hate. I think it turns us all into demons. You know?"

"I get you," Jacob said, but he thought it was kind of hard not to hate his captors. "So, why do they call you Whistler?"

"Because I whistle a lot. Well, I used to. Kind of lost my voice a bit in here."

"That's not the real reason for the name, is it?"

"No, just thought you'd appreciate the humour. I got the name because I blow the whistle on the demons. I can see them, see who they really are. I alert the Order when we've got an infiltration. Well, Daniel excluded."

"So what's your real name then?"

"Brogan," Whistler said. "I never asked you yours."

"Jacob."

"Cool. Sounds better than mine. Do you have a smuggler name?"

"No. People just call me Jacob."

"That's a little boring, don't you think?"

Jacob laughed. "I suppose it is."

"See, I knew you'd like the humour." He paused and scratched his head, leaving his long, curled hair sticking up. "How about Spider?"

"What, because I crawl around?"

"No, because you've got lanky legs," Whistler said with a grin.

"Yes, but only two of them."

"True," Whistler said. "But your name's Jacob. Cob, an old word for spider. You know?"

"Yes, I guess I do," Jacob said, nodding.

* * *

A guard passed by, silencing them with his presence. Jacob almost wanted to hurl insults at the man. In prison, words could still fit through the bars. Though it was a great effort, the thought of Whistler sharing his beating stopped his usually rampant tongue.

"They come by every hour," Whistler whispered.

"Say what you want about the Regime," Jacob said. "They're diligent."

The words of his father returned like a phantom. *They are like you and I.* Jacob wondered if that was what made them dangerous.

"Some of them throw in bread and water," Whistler said. "I wouldn't eat it though."

Jacob did not think the youth ever had. Whistler had wasted away while the demon soldiers grew fat. It brought back that unnerving thought: *In time they will replace us.*

He could never quite get his father's words out of his head. They lingered there like a lodger. Perhaps it was because his father drilled them in daily. It was his own regime.

Jacob adjusted his position to squint at the guard as he faded into the distance, and then Jacob felt something in his back pocket. He held it up to the paltry light, which showed the iron currency, a flattened coil stamped with the image of the Iron Emperor. Jacob flicked it into the air, and caught it in his hand. There was something reassuring about it, even though there was something very unsettling about the visage upon it.

"I don't think they do room service," Whistler said.

Jacob reached for the mouldy bread. "Sure they do."

For hours they talked, Jacob telling Whistler about his adventures smuggling amulets into the city of Blackout, and how even the mayor's daughter wanted one, but cancelled the deal at the last minute out of fear of being caught by her father.

Whistler told Jacob about the Order, how it was struggling to keep up production of the amulets and was running out of Magi to enchant them. He hinted that the Order was planning something big, that it had a hidden weapon against the Regime.

The hours passed, or perhaps it was days, but the two kept chatting until they no longer had the energy to speak. The stale bread grew staler, and Jacob often looked to it when his stomach had a voice of its own. His sleep was restless, broken by the clutching cold, disrupted by the screams and wails of other prisoners for whom the Hold was home.

As the days passed, Jacob thought long about the name of his prison. He began to wonder if now that it had its grip, it would ever let go.

A clang of metal seized Jacob from his sleep. He could hear footsteps approaching, could see a lantern coming closer through his grit-covered eyes.

A panic took hold of him, clenching his lungs and tightening his throat. They were here for Whistler or for him, but either way it was not good. Someone was getting tortured this night, or maybe the guards would have mercy and send them straight to the headman's axe.

As the fear gnawed at his thoughts, he found himself praying to everyone else's god, half-heartedly apologising for his sins and half-earnestly begging for mercy. Yet when the devils came, he knew that he would ask for none.

The thumping boots sounded louder, each thud like a hammer against his pounding heart. The light of the lantern made the shadows of the figures dance across the walls, like taunting phantoms, like mocking demons.

Then a hand reached out for the lock on the final gate. A flash of light illuminated the room for a second, where he could see Whistler curled up once again in the corner, no longer hidden from sight.

The gate swung open, and the sound was like Death speaking. Three figures stood there, hooded and cloaked, perhaps the emissaries of Death himself.

The tallest figure stepped forward and pulled down its hood. It was a woman with fiery long hair, locks that seemed to flicker just like the candle flames. Her eyes were stern, boring through the shadow like little lanterns of their own.

"Taberah!" Whistler cried.

"It's time to get you out of here, Brogan," the woman said.

Jacob no longer held his breath. They were not here for him. They were not his captors—but they were not his saviours either.

Chapter Two

THE BREAKOUT

"Who is this?" Taberah asked. She looked at Jacob as if he were Whistler's new-found pet, some scruffy dog he had picked up from the streets. It was not a completely unwarranted description.

"Jacob," Whistler said. "He's a smuggler." *Can we keep him?* Jacob almost heard him say.

Taberah turned to the cowled man to her left. "Kill him. We don't need any witnesses."

The man took out a pistol, which glinted in the candlelight, stinging Jacob's eyes before the bullets would sting his body. *So I guess I'm to be put down.* Compared to what the Regime would do, Jacob almost did not mind.

"No!" Whistler cried, struggling to stand up. Taberah caught him as he began to fall.

"Please, Taberah," Whistler begged. "Let him live."

Taberah's eyes softened as she studied Jacob. Perhaps his rough demeanour, his ragged blonde hair, his tangle of a beard, and his feigned puppy dog eyes helped lower her guard. He was just a stray caught by the pound.

It was clear that Taberah was debating with

herself. Perhaps a part of her had pity, but if it did, it was a buried part, and it took long to unearth.

"We don't have time for this," the cowled man said. Jacob hoped they did not have time to kill him either.

"Let's go," Taberah said, and she turned and rushed into the darkness like a flame snatched by the wind. The others followed, dragging Whistler with them.

Jacob was not entirely sure if he should immediately pursue them, but then he saw Whistler smile and beckon to him as he was hauled down the corridor. Clearly this was Taberah's roundabout way of letting Jacob join the pack. They were not taking him with them, but he was going to follow them home.

Jacob limped after them, his right hand against the wall for support. Pain shot through his legs and into his back, while the light threatened to stab out his eyes with its blinding glare. He had not quite realised how much the Hold had taken out of him, and he wondered if maybe he might not make it home at all.

Often he tripped over stones or loose tiles, and less often over the bodies of the Regime's guards. When his eyes adjusted to the light, he began to realise the brutality that had been used on them. Some were limbless and headless, their corpses butchered and mangled. The walls were painted red, which Jacob soon realised when he placed his hands upon them. He began to wish for the stabbing light again.

Taberah stormed ahead, her boots splashing in the pools of blood, her thick hair trailing behind her like blood-coloured serpents. Whistler was being carried by the cowled man now, who Jacob assumed was one of the Order's soldiers, but so little was known of the group that he could not really tell. Onwards they hurried, the other hooded figure stopping every now and then to run a dagger through a dying guard's throat.

Jacob struggled to keep up, his limbs weak and his mind weighing him down with the worries of what might lie ahead. Taberah and her people did not look back and did not slow down for him. Jacob knew well that if it were not for Whistler he would have been left behind, or more likely his blood would have given the walls a second coating.

The prison was like a maze, twisting this way and that, with many corridors, many doors, and many more cages. Whispers seemed to come from the walls, or perhaps they were from some other withering prisoners. Jacob did not know which thought creeped him out more.

Suddenly he bumped into one of the Order soldiers, and he realised that they had all halted, with guns at the ready. The soldier who was carrying Whistler handed the boy to Jacob. Though Jacob did not have his full strength back, the child was very light—a little too light.

"What are we waiting for?" Jacob whispered.

Whistler nodded in Taberah's direction. She was slowly sliding a small mirror around the corner. It had barely gotten an inch around before it smashed as a bullet hit it.

"I guess there's someone around there then,"

Jacob said.

Taberah glowered at him. Maybe he should not have barked at all.

One of the Order soldiers leapt around the corner, shooting as he went, despite Taberah trying to hold him back. He was killed in seconds.

Taberah took a grenade from her belt, a belt with many more weapons attached, and pulled the pin. She cast it around the corner, despite her fallen comrade being there. There was a loud explosion, and many cries, and Jacob was thankful that the dust disguised the blood.

"*Now* you can go, Soasa," Taberah said to the other soldier, who was less than willing. Her glare gave the cowled woman courage enough, and she ran around the corner, rifle in hand. Taberah followed, and Jacob, with Whistler in his arms, hurried after her.

There must have been half a dozen Regime guards dead upon the ground, some of them in half a dozen pieces. Jacob wished he did not have to look to the floor to mind his step, and he noticed that Whistler was staring at the ceiling, which was not entirely red.

They continued through the corridors, past many other cells. Jacob was almost tempted to ask if they could free them, but he had a feeling that Taberah had adopted enough mutts tonight. As they ran, Jacob adjusted and threw Whistler over his shoulder.

"Sorry, kid," he said to Whistler's protestations. "I think it's best if I have a hand free." He hoped he would not need it.

They slowed down as Taberah surveyed the next

junction. Another mirror, but this one did not break.

"You could give me a weapon, you know," Jacob said. "You've got enough of them."

She threw him a small knife.

Jacob scoffed. "Thanks."

"You can pay for it later," she said.

Jacob remembered the coil in his pocket. This knife was not even worth that much. "Maybe I'll pay for it now," he said.

"Later," she repeated, more forcefully.

She began to pick up the pace, employing less tact and guile. Jacob had mixed feelings about that. On on hand, it must have meant they were close to an exit, but on the other hand they might not make it out at all if they were not careful. They turned corner after corner, left and right, right and left, until it seemed to Jacob that maybe they were going in circles. Each time he caught up with Taberah she would vanish around another corner, and if it were not for him carrying Whistler he might have thought she did not want him to find her at all.

He heard shouts from behind him. "Halt or we'll shoot!" the Regime guards cried, but he did not halt, and they did not go back on their word. A barrage of bullets came his way, but he swung around a corner just in time, passing by Soasa, who quickly laid explosives on the floor. She had barely re-joined him when he heard the bombs go off, followed by a tumble of bricks and a tumult of screams. While neither Taberah nor Soasa were exactly on his side, he was glad they were not his enemies.

"Impressive," Jacob said to Soasa. She ignored

him.

A few more twists and turns brought them to an exit, of which Soasa made short work. The brightness of the morning sun flooded the corridor like an invasion, seizing every eye. Despite its oppressive glare, they welcomed it eagerly, for they had lived under the oppression of the darkness for long enough.

A waft of fresh air tickled Jacob's nose and filled his lungs for what seemed like the first time in his life. He could taste it on his tongue, fresh and pure. Often prisoners said they could taste freedom and Jacob dismissed it, but now he knew it was true—and it tasted good.

They stood close to the exit for a moment, covering their eyes from the sun. Jacob could barely make out anything but red sands in one direction and yellow sands in another.

Taberah looked left and right several times, as if a second glance might summon something into sight. "It isn't here," she grumbled.

"What are we looking for?" Jacob asked.

"It's supposed to be here," she said. Her exasperation was palpable. She might have had the skill to get them out of the Hold, but who knew how she would fare across the empty deserts of Altadas. Jacob was almost certain that Whistler would not survive the journey.

Suddenly a huge silver warwagon sped into view, halting in a whirl of dust. The door opened, and a fat, bald man offered his hand.

"Sorry," the man said. "We were a bit delayed."

"A bit, Teller," she said, and her eyes almost

impaled him.

Soasa took Whistler from Jacob and bundled him on board. Taberah followed swiftly.

Jacob gasped for breath, wondering if they would roll off without him, but then he thought he heard his name and looked up to see Taberah peering through one of the wagon's windows. "Get in," she ordered. He did not like that it was an order, and part of him felt like defying her. He did not feel like that for long.

Jacob hobbled up to the wagon and clambered aboard, where he collapsed upon the ground. The people inside looked at him in disgust, as if he truly were some wild dog that had come in from the mud. If it was not condemning glares, it was dismissive glances.

Jacob feigned a smile. *Maybe I should have stayed at the pound.*

Chapter Three

THE PLOT

The warwagon sped off almost before Jacob had both legs inside. Teller slammed the door shut and reached down to tap Jacob's shoes with his greasy hands.

"Mind your feet," he said. Were it not for his soft voice and helpful eyes, greatly magnified by his immense glasses, Jacob might have thought he was being sarcastic.

Jacob wanted to rest for a moment on the floor, but he did not like the stares of all the strangers around him, nor their muttered words about him. He clambered up and looked around. This vehicle, dubbed the Silver Ghost, was very different to the ones the Regime used. For a start, it was much bigger, with what looked like several rooms and corridors, and the predominant metal was silver, and the predominant adornment was red silk. To Jacob's eyes it was lavish, which contrasted starkly with the minimalist decor that the Regime employed.

"So," Jacob said as he tried to figure out where to go. "Which way did Taberah go?"

The stares grew more intense, and those who were not staring were looking at each other with incredulity, as if the dog just talked. *Okay*, Jacob thought. *I'll find my own way*. At the last moment he saw Soasa further down the corridor and headed in her direction.

"A friendly lot," he said.

"To friends, yes," she replied.

"I wonder how you treat enemies."

"You already know," she said, and she took several sticks of dynamite and sealed them in a chest.

"Remind me not to become your enemy."

"I don't think you need the reminder."

"An explosive tongue," he said.

She glanced at him, but did not respond, as if she also knew how not to light the fuse.

"So, you wouldn't happen to know where I can find Taberah?" he asked.

"She'll find you."

At that moment Taberah came out of the room further down the corridor, her scarlet coat flowing beneath her scarlet hair.

"Speak of the devil," Jacob said.

"On this warwagon, there's only one devil," Taberah said.

Jacob smiled. "If you mean me, then maybe I wouldn't have needed rescuing."

"Are you really bringing this?" Soasa asked Taberah, as if Jacob was not even there.

This? Jacob thought. *So much for all I've done for the Order*. It was not entirely true. He had mostly done it for himself.

Taberah rolled her eyes. "He's for the boy," she said. "A toy, if you will."

"A smuggler is a dangerous toy," Soasa said.

"And dynamite isn't?" Jacob quizzed.

"They do not care for the Order," Soasa continued, ignoring him. "It is all about the coils."

"Yes," Taberah acknowledged, "but Brogan has a knack for these kinds of things. I trust his instinct by now and you should trust my judgement."

That was enough for Soasa to take the hint and walk away. Jacob noticed that she gave no nod or salute, no acknowledgement of Taberah's superior rank, if indeed she was superior at all.

"If I didn't need her," Taberah quipped, "I would drop her quicker than I drop smugglers."

"That's nice to know," Jacob said, resting his back against the cool silver walls. He was glad it was a different metal; the memory of being bundled into the Regime's iron wagon was still very near. Perhaps it did not live in his mind, but in his bones.

"Jacob," Taberah said, toying with his name. "It's a rather funny name."

"Some call me Spider," Jacob said with a smile.

"Oh? Well, it looks like the spider got caught in his own web. How is that?"

"I was looking for too many flies."

Taberah smiled. "Why does Brogan think you might be useful?"

"Because I might be," Jacob said.

"You've yet to tell me how."

"You've yet to tell me what you need."

"So you're a jack of all trades then," she said. It was true to some degree. Jacob had dabbled in anything he could get his hands on, often risking his own hands in the process. He had tried to make weapons and armour, could drive almost anything, had even tried his hand at picking enchanted locks, only to find out that he probably needed lessons as a Magus as well.

"I do this and that," Jacob said, which was true, but he knew that Taberah probably had a different interpretation of the phrase than he had.

"We need a man like that," she said. "We lost our handyman while rescuing Brogan. His body is probably somewhere in the Hold."

"That's a reassuring job offer," Jacob said. "I hope you pay up front."

"It's much more reassuring than the alternative, Jacob." Jacob knew what that meant. He felt caught between the Regime and the Order, and their war. It did not matter if he was neutral in the no man's land—he could still be killed in the crossfire.

"Tell me what you need. If it's delivering amulets, I've got good references."

"If it was delivering amulets you wouldn't be in my warwagon," Taberah snapped. "This isn't the time for this anyway. We all need rest, Brogan more than any of us. Go find an empty room and sleep. You really will need it."

Jacob gave a mocking salute and began searching for a room. Taberah's command made him realise just how badly he needed sleep, as if she had cast a curse upon him.

He knocked on several doors, resulting in many angry shouts. On one occasion he heard no response, so he ended up walking in on a woman undressing.

She chased him out, bashing him with her shoe.

"I didn't see anything!" he cried as he shielded his head. "Not much to see," he added beneath his breath.

She slammed the door, and Jacob turned around to find Teller standing there, as if waiting in line to barge in on the woman changing.

"Hell," Jacob said. "Do you have to creep up on people like that?"

"Oh, do not mind me," Teller said, fidgeting with his enormous glasses as he spoke. "Take this room. No one is using it." He led Jacob to a room further down the hall.

"Thanks," Jacob said.

"A little courtesy goes a long way," Teller said with a slimy smile.

"Yes, I guess it does."

Before Jacob entered his quarters, he passed another room with the door wide open. He glanced inside and saw Whistler sleeping, but his head turned this way and that as if he were caught in the clutches of a nightmare. A doctor sat beside his bed, bathing his head with a damp cloth, and clutching a deck of cards in his other hand, as if the boy had fallen asleep mid-game. In the strong light of the lanterns Jacob could see how gaunt the youth appeared. He also saw for the first time the wounds of torture on his body: cruel cuts, brutal bruises, and barbaric burns. He worried if Whistler would survive whatever fought him in his dreams.

"Poor thing," Teller said, peering over Jacob's shoulder. Jacob could not help but cringe.

"Yes," he said. "Well, good night."

Jacob might have waited for the doctor to come out, to see how Whistler was doing, but Teller's unsettling presence encouraged him to go quickly into his room and lock the door. For a while he almost thought he heard Teller's breathing outside, and he wondered if maybe he would guard his door all night. *Helpful*, Jacob thought. *Too helpful.*

Then Jacob finally succumbed to the growing weight of his body and his eyelids, his face hitting the soft feather pillow and his mind drifting off to where strange things made sense.

When morning came, Jacob found that Whistler was up bright and early—too early—and insisted on waking him. He banged at the door until Jacob reluctantly unlocked it. Jacob almost expected to see Teller there instead.

"You should be resting, Whistler," Jacob said. Perhaps he meant: *I should be resting.* "You were in the Hold much longer than I was. You need to build up your strength again."

"I'm feeling much better," Whistler said. He looked better, but he was still very thin and weak. A single night's recuperation was not going to be enough to mend his trauma. Jacob wondered if anything could.

"So am I," Jacob said, stretching and yawning. "It's amazing what a good night's rest can do, or rather what a bed made for kings can do. I'm too used to sleeping rough. A smuggler's life is far from an elegant one."

"Why did you become a smuggler?" Whistler asked, sitting down on a nearby chair and running his fingers through his hair. His hair looked much better now that it had been washed. It appeared that the doctor had also cut it to just above his shoulders, where it hung in long reddish-brown curls. Jacob felt his own hair could do with a trim; he was not used to letting it grow wild, even if it was nowhere near the length of Whistler's. He thought he could do with a shave too.

"A lack of options, I guess," Jacob replied. "My father never wanted me to become a smuggler. He always told me to do my studies, to try harder. I always defied him. If he had told me to become a smuggler, then maybe I wouldn't be today."

"So it's his fault?" Whistler asked. If it was not for the boy's curious expression Jacob might have thought he was trying to make a point.

"Well, no, not exactly," Jacob said. "A job's a job."

"I didn't have much of a choice either," Whistler said, biting his lip. "I was kind of born into the Order. But that's better than what could have been. It freaks me out thinking about all those births with the Regime pulling the strings. I can barely imagine what it must be like for a mother to know that the Regime had put a demon inside her, that she couldn't really have a proper baby."

"Well, that's what the amulets are for, right?" Jacob said.

"Yeah, but they only block the channel. They don't make the babies real."

"There's nothing that can do that now," Jacob said

solemnly.

"The Pure can," Whistler suggested enthusiastically.

It took great effort on Jacob's part not to scoff. It was all a fairy tale, something to give people hope. Without it, they might not have fought this war for fifteen years. They might stop fighting altogether. There were no such things as angels, but the demons were very real.

"It's a pity the amulets only stop the demons being born," Whistler said. "How do we fight off the thousands that are already here?"

"The same way we fight off our own kind," Jacob said. "With guns. Preferably big guns. If we can distinguish them from the rest of us in the first place, that is."

"That's why I'm here," Whistler said, tilting his head and smiling sheepishly.

Jacob spent much of the morning queuing for the bathroom, much to the obvious dissatisfaction of other Order members, who made sure to get in before him. He shaved his beard and trimmed his hair. Doctor Mudro offered to give him a full haircut, revealing a possible career as a barber as well as a surgeon and stage magician, but Jacob refused. He did not like the idea of someone else cutting his hair. It did not have to be perfect. It just had to not block his eyes during any of his odd jobs.

As he stared into the mirror, he thought: *Thirty-five years gone. Let's hope for another thirty-five.* He took this time to also give his clothes a scrub. The dark brown leather was still covered in dirt from the Hold, and soot from Blackout, the city that had earned its name from its oppressive smog. Many complained about it, but it was something he quite liked. It helped the smuggling trade to no end.

As Jacob cleaned himself up, and almost felt like he was staying in a hotel, he glanced time and time again in the mirror, and shuddered. He half expected to see Teller standing behind him, ready to hand him a towel or compliment his hairdo. But there was no one there, which left more room for Jacob's imagination.

Later that day everyone in the Order's warwagon was summoned to a meeting with Taberah, who sat like a queen on her throne observing her people. Jacob hung at the back, and Whistler stayed with him. Jacob preferred to stay in the shadows, out of sight and mind, but the strong glare of Taberah confirmed that he was being closely watched.

"We have fulfilled our mission to get Whistler back," Taberah said, which was met with a cheer. Everyone looked at Whistler, and suddenly Jacob realised they were also staring at him. He tried to shrink further into the shadows.

"But we have lost many in our plight," Taberah continued, "and the Resistance is under threat. Every night they raid one of our havens, and every night they kill more of our people. Meanwhile the ranks of the demons grow, unbridled by our attempts to stop them with the amulets.

"The Regime has outlawed our amulets because they will stop people conceiving. They have told the people that we are committing sins, killing the unborn. But they are deceivers, for they control the channels of birth, and through them they send the souls of demons who desire corporeal form. Through *our* women they are born, defiling our people, pretending to be our children, yet always waiting to hand us in.

"That's why we need a final answer. This world is not the natural home of the Regime, and those demons cannot survive here without the constant use of Hope. It's their drug, and the Hope factories are their dealers. We'll target the Hope factory near Blackout, and we'll make certain it can never produce Hope again. It's time we hit them where it hurts. It's them to starve them out."

Chapter Four

CONFIDANTE

There was much commotion following Taberah's announcement, and she spent most of that day answering questions, and eventually refusing to meet with anyone else.

Jacob loitered in the corridors again, proudly making a nuisance of himself. He passed by Soasa, who refused to make way for him. He tried to nudge past, much to her vocal displeasure.

"You're in my way," she growled.

"You're in mine," Jacob replied. "Maybe we can share it," he added with a cheeky grin.

"All of this belongs to the Order," she said. "Even you."

"In all my years as a smuggler for you lot, I never saw that in the job description."

This time Soasa tried to push through, but Jacob blocked her path. She stepped to his left, and he followed, and she stepped to his right, and he met her there as well. It was the kind of dance that everybody knew.

"This cart might have many rooms," Jacob said, "but the corridors are tiny."

"Would you not rather have the vastness of the

desert?" Soasa said. "You could sleep outside."

"I like it cosy," Jacob said. "This'll do just fine."

"Move," she barked.

But Jacob was immovable, and his smile was dauntless. "Unless, of course, you want to make it cosier."

"I'd rather die," she said.

"Keep playing with dynamite and you just might."

She pushed past like an explosion, and he did not resist. She shook her head as she walked on, perhaps to remove even the memory of him, but he fancied that maybe she was smiling anyway. She was not.

Soasa continued on to Taberah's room, barging in without knocking. It was something Taberah had grown used to, despite numerous meetings on the matter.

"You brought a pest on board," Soasa hissed, like the sound of her fuse wearing thin.

"A pet," Taberah corrected. She continued making notes in her diary as if Soasa had not disturbed her. She looked up from the book and added, "Does he bother you that much?"

"Yes," Soasa said. "You shouldn't give him free rein."

"I'll do what I like."

Soasa looked as though she was fighting back her own tongue. "You always do," she said at last.

"Do you have a problem with me, Soasa?"

"I have a problem with *him*."

"Then sort it out. As it stands, he might be useful."

"As a plaything for the boy?" Soasa remarked.

"Are you sure he's not yours?"

"I don't have playthings," Taberah replied coldly. She no longer looked at her diary; she kept her eyes firmly on Soasa, as if she were writing in her soul.

Soasa scoffed. "Sure. And how did you end up with the boy in the first place?"

"Get out," Taberah said, standing up, "or I'll throw you out ... and I don't just mean the room."

"He came on to *me*, you know, but I refused him. I don't sleep with anyone and everyone to get my way. You might think it, but he's not interested in you."

"We'll see," Taberah said.

It was approaching midnight when Jacob received an invitation to meet with Taberah privately in her quarters. It was only the second night in his own, but he was already restless. He spent more time roaming the corridors, getting in everyone's way. He somewhat enjoyed it.

If Taberah's invitation had been an order instead, he might have refused. As it stood, he contemplated delaying a bit, to arrive on his own time, if not his own terms. Boredom overcame his conviction, however, and he strolled through the corridors to Taberah's room, making sure to smile at everyone he passed, few of whom smiled in return. He was surprised so many were up at this time. It seemed the Order never slept.

He saw that Taberah's door was slightly ajar, but he knocked anyway before peering in.

"Anyone at home?" he asked.

"Come in," she said. "And shut the door behind

you."

"Yes, ma'am," he said, his vocal salute.

"Don't call me that."

"What shall I call you?" he asked as he quietly closed the door.

"By my name," Taberah said, standing up and walking over to Jacob until their faces were but inches apart. "It is customary after all."

Her eyes sparkled. Her lips shimmered. She wore her hair up in a bun, which was fixed with four sticks, one vertical and three horizontal, forming the sigil of the Order. She wore a scarlet dress, and her lips were painted to match. She looked less like a rebel leader now and more like a queen. Jacob wondered if she would come into power if the Regime was overthrown.

She walked back to her dresser, where she put a final note in her diary, before hiding it in one of the drawers.

"I keep a record of everything we do," she said. "Every detail."

"What did you put in about me?" Jacob asked.

"Not much," she replied. "I don't know enough about you yet."

"I'm pretty much an open book. What you see is what you get."

"Disappointing," she said. "I was hoping there was more."

"I might have a few more surprises."

"I don't like surprises," she said. "In this world, surprises can kill you."

"Or make you feel alive."

She approached Jacob again and placed her right hand upon his chest, over his heart, as if to see if he really had a heart. Some said the demons did not. It would explain many of their atrocities.

"It seems Whistler has taken quite a shine to you," Taberah said as she withdrew.

"Well, what can I say? I'm great."

Taberah smiled. "I doubt the Regime would agree."

"I doubt the Regime would be singing praises about you either."

"No, that's true," Taberah said.

"It looks like Whistler's the only one who likes me here."

"Perhaps." She circled around him like a serpent. "How many amulets have you smuggled into Blackout?"

"I've lost count," Jacob said. "A few hundred, maybe."

"And the money you got? Have you lost count of that?"

Jacob grinned. "Not quite. I'm a bit of a hoarder, you might say."

"Do you hoard it because it's money or because it's iron?"

"Black gold? The Regime's holy treasure?"

"Precisely."

"I hoarded real gold when that was worth anything," he explained. "If the currency had changed to sugar cubes, I might have opened a candy shop."

"I can't see you as a shopkeeper," she remarked. "Too stable, too legitimate."

"I told you I was an open book."

"Not open enough."

"This is starting to feel like an interrogation," he said. "Are you trying to see if I'm an informer? Surely Whistler would know."

"He's been wrong before."

"Well, read me from cover to cover," Jacob said. "I have no allegiance to the Regime."

"And to the Order? To the Resistance?"

"I have none either," he stated.

"It's hard to remain neutral in this war."

"Then add that as another skill to my resume," he said. "Or to your record of me in your diary. I might like to read it one day."

"Wishful thinking," she replied.

Taberah walked to the dresser and looked into the mirror. She took the wooden sticks out of her hair one by one, until her hair cascaded down her head and shoulders like lava. She turned her head to look at Jacob, and as she did the right strap of her dress slipped from her shoulder.

"You're quite a woman, you know," Jacob said.

"I know," Taberah said. She sat down on her bed, her head tilted to the side, her hair cast behind her back to reveal her naked shoulder.

"If I were a wiser man I'd think you were trying to seduce me," Jacob said.

"Then perhaps you are a wise man," Taberah said as she ran her hand down her leg, all the while staring at Jacob with an inviting gaze.

Jacob closed his eyes for a second, wondering what he was doing, if this was really happening. He did not know why she wanted him, and yet he did not know why he wanted her, but he felt a carnal hunger, needed to feel her fiery touch.

"It won't be safe," he said at last, trying to control himself. The words were a struggle, fighting with his tongue as he tried to speak.

She smiled, running her hand across her breasts, revealing the amulet she wore. "A smuggler isn't afraid of getting a little dirty, is he?"

Jacob could no longer resist her lure. He grabbed her arms and pulled her to him, even as he pushed himself against her. They collapsed upon the bed, where Taberah's hair flayed out like a peacock's tail. She dug her nails into the muscles on his arms. He kissed her neck, which smelled of a strong perfume, and ran his hands across her thighs. Their bodies were warm, their breathing shallow. The night brought darkness, and it brought pleasure.

Taberah lay upon her back, clutching the bed sheets as if they might suddenly disappear. She stared at the ceiling, unable to sleep. Her breathing was still shallow, but her mind was deep with restless thoughts. She glanced at the window, where a sliver of moonlight leaked into the room. The night had deepened.

She turned to her left, where Jacob slept. His face was buried in a pillow, but it did little to muffle his monstrous snores. Taberah prodded him to see if he was really sleeping. He did not budge. Then she rolled out of the bed and put on her night coat, which lay on a nearby chair. She walked towards the dresser, holding firmly the tie that held the night coat closed.

When she reached the dresser she paused and ran her hand down her chest until it met with the amulet she wore. She grabbed and held it for a moment, feeling the warmth that emanated from deep within. With her other hand she reached around the back of her neck and grabbed the chain. She took the amulet off and held it up to the moonlight, where it sparkled. Then she opened a drawer in the dresser and placed it deep inside its shadows, where no moon could reveal the long crack that ran down the length of its fragile glass.

Chapter Five

SCOUTING PARTY

Given Taberah's apparent impulsiveness, Jacob expected their first visit to the Hope factory to be the final assault. Instead, after receiving a telegram from a friend, she organised a small group for a scouting mission, and Jacob was not at all surprised to be included. Whistler, however, was not among that number.

"I want to come with you," Whistler said.

"No," Taberah replied. "This is a mission for the few, and those few should be able to fight."

"I can fight."

"Fight and win," Taberah said.

Whistler looked disheartened. Taberah was less comforting than Jacob would have been.

"We all have different skills," Jacob said, trying his best to console Whistler. "You have valuable skills that I don't have, so I don't think Taberah can risk you getting killed."

"Or caught again," Whistler said.

The scouting party was small in number, with just Taberah, Jacob, and six other Order soldiers, none of whom Jacob recognised. As far as Jacob was concerned, it was six people, maybe even seven, too many. There was a reason why scouts often went alone, and he knew from experience that solitude was the friend of the smuggler, and was undoubtedly on good terms with the scout as well.

Taberah arranged for them to be taken by the Silver Ghost as close as possible to the nearest Hope factory, just south of the central city of Blackout, and from there they would be alone to conduct their perilous survey. Jacob noticed the growing apprehension on the faces of the others, even those who would not be going on that journey, for even treading close to the Regime's prized production facilities was a monumental danger.

As they drew closer, Taberah studied an old map. The majority of the Hope factories were built in the industrial heart of Altadas, deep in the craggy workshops of the mining towns that spanned the Iron Mountains to the far east. The primary factory, which produced the most Hope, and presumably had the most guards, was in the town of Rockhold, now called Hopehaven, and the miners were converted to the religion of slavery, where pickaxes and shovels were the tools of their daily ritual, and they prayed always to the Iron Emperor, and they gave a tithing to the Regime with their blood, sweat and tears.

There was something about slavery that bothered Jacob more than many other forms of oppression, even death. He did not like the idea of working to further the goal of evil, to help enslave others. In those kinds of factories, humans were the machines.

* * *

The Hope factory was menacing in the distance, for it was one of the few buildings that somehow managed to present itself through the smog. Its hulking form consumed almost all of the horizon, and its many pistons, pillars, chimneys and flumes ate into the heavens. For the parts of the sky it could not reach, those towers sent up endless streams of smoke, and this smoke devoured the natural clouds and left an unnatural haze in the heavens. The factory was a greedy mass of brick, a ravenous form of iron. As much as it gobbled up all the landscape, it threatened that it might eat the onlookers too.

It grew by the week, for the demons grew in number, and they needed sustenance, and so they stole the land and the sky, and they replaced it with concrete, steel and iron, until the very building mirrored the multiplication of the demonic horde. For now the world of Altadas was mostly an empty desert, but in the future it might be a world of iron.

Who knew that in those bleak walls, darkened by soot, corroded by gas, there was something produced that was so brilliantly white in substance? To those who dwelt inside the factory, for they did not work there so much as live there, the product of their labour must have seemed like a nectar of the gods. In such a grim location, there was little wonder that they called the powder Hope.

"I'm having second thoughts now," Whistler said, and perhaps he was thankful that the tangle of his hair blocked out some of the sombre sight before him.

"You wanted adventure," Taberah said. "This is it."

"There's no fun without a bit of risk," Jacob said, but he was hoping it would not just be him that risked his life.

The Silver Ghost halted, and they knew that the mission of many had passed to the sortie of a few. A hasty farewell was shared, and they departed as the sky grew dim, darkened now not only by the night, but by the Hope factory's noxious fumes.

"I hope you brought your sketch book," Jacob said. "That's a big factory to survey."

"I have," Taberah said, holding up a notepad, "but we also have something else." She tapped her foot against a large box with a pinhole in one end and a curtain on the other. "It's called a dark chamber, and it produces pictures almost like what the eye can see."

It took two miles of creeping to come close enough to the Hope factory to inspect its defences. At times Jacob thought he saw figures ahead, or behind, or to either side of him, but Taberah tried to reassure him that no one was there. How she knew, she would not say.

The Hope factory was far better defended than they had thought. What at a distance merged into one great mass, now up close became a series of obstacles to any attacker. The building, or perhaps it was a family of buildings, giving birth to more ugly cubes of concrete every week, was surrounded by ditches, trenches, and barbed wire, and for those who managed to get through those defences, while evading the many searchlights and machine gun fire, there were towers that did not produce steam or smoke, but billowed bullets. Around the walls marched many troops, and they might have even seemed human were it not for their almost unnatural uniformity, their unsettling discipline. Further still, there were numerous machines on wheels and tracks and treads, pushed and powered by steam, creaking and heaving as they moved, dripping oil, the blood of industrial war.

"This is more than I expected," Taberah admitted.

"I thought the Order was all-powerful?" Jacob jested.

"If we were, we would rule this world, not the Regime." From the tone of her voice, Jacob could tell that she was not joking.

Taberah crawled closer to those deadly defences, and Jacob winced more and more with each movement she made. "I need a better view," she whispered, and Jacob reluctantly followed, hoping this better view would not be their last one.

Taberah hurriedly scrawled pictures and notes of the factory in her notebook, while one of the soldiers employed the dark chamber, burying his head beneath the curtain, as if he was trying to hide from sight. What images he saw, and how they would turn out, was anyone's guess, but the image that Jacob saw frightened him, and he could not help but feel that someone was watching back.

Suddenly a spotlight shone upon them, and some of them froze, as if the light were some kind of prison. Yet the freedom of darkness was a haven for Taberah and Jacob, both of whom had learned by now how to swiftly flee into its depths.

A hail of bullets fell upon those who did not leave the spotlight in time, and the white light turned to red. There were screams and scouts, and the sounds of heavy boots, grinding cogs, and screeching steel. Spotlights appeared by the dozen, like the bullets of heaven's gun, and anyone caught running through one of them did not run for long.

Jacob's heart pounded as if it was firing its own bullets of blood through every artery. He scrambled low across the ground, hiding deep in the darkness, as far away from the searchlights as he could get. He could not see Taberah or anyone else from the scouting party, and though part of him felt exposed away from that group, another part thought that he might be better off alone. He never joined the various smuggler guilds that operated throughout the region, because he always felt that larger groups made better targets. He lived alone and he smuggled alone. Now he tried to smuggle himself out of the line of fire.

He paused for a moment to survey his surroundings. The dark was oppressing where he hid, but he was glad that it was his only oppressor, and that it was as much an ally, for if he could not see his own hands before him, then the Regime could not see them either. The spotlights lit up parts of the land further ahead and behind him, and they moved slowly around, illuminating regiments of heavily-armed troops, and, most frightening of all, great war machines powered by steam and cog, rolling on great wheels, moving on tracks and treads, or even stomping down on steel and iron legs. Many of those were only half-revealed by the light, for they were big in size, and the spotlights, though huge, were not big enough to contain them.

Jacob decided that he had to act quick if he was to avoid detection, for he knew the Regime would sweep the entire area, and he did not want to be swept away by its landships. He turned away from the war machines and began to crawl through the darkness on the other side, where he presumed, and hoped, he must have come from.

A spotlight edged dangerously close to him, and he managed to roll away just in time. Then another came near, but it backed off before seizing his silhouette. In time Jacob found that he was almost surrounded by them, as if they in some way sensed roughly where he was, and were closing in like the iron bars of his even darker cell in the Hold. Ahead of him he saw two larger spotlights standing still like pillars, between which was a tiny sliver of darkness, maybe just big enough to fit through. Everywhere else was blocked off, or led back towards the war machines, and Jacob realised that these pillars marked his only doorway, his exit to safety, or the entrance of a new kind of cell.

Every smuggler was in some way a gambler, and every job was a gamble with their life, so Jacob knew the lure of chance, and the thrill of risk, but he also knew the paralysis of fear, which almost held him long enough for another spotlight to pass over him. He dodged it and leapt forward, into that thin channel of darkness, and he crawled between the two glares, like the soul might crawl between the twin lights of life and death. He kept his eyes ahead, for the light on either side was blinding, and he felt an irrational fear that looking too much into its sheen might lure him into it. He continued on, with safety only moments away.

Suddenly he realised that his left baby finger was ever so slightly illuminated, and he froze for a second before realising that the light on either side was closing slowly in on him. He carefully stepped up and turned sideways to fit in the ever dwindling strip of darkness. He edged along, even as the lights edged closer to him. His heart began to pound louder, and his mouth was terribly dry, and his palms were terribly wet. He began to make out a little more of his own figure, and thrill turned to terror, and he felt the urge to close his eyes and brace his body for what undoubtedly would be a quick, but not in any way painless, death. He defied this urge, however, and he sidled more quickly through the vanishing darkness, until finally, just as the light from one spotlight merged into the other, he leapt out of the way and into the greater darkness beyond, and he collapsed on the ground, where he panted and pounded away from prying eyes.

Suddenly a hand seized his shoulder, and he might have leapt back into the danger of those lights if he had not realised in time that it was Taberah, who seemed well suited to the shadow, which was perhaps even more a home to her than it was to Jacob.

"You're lucky I found you," Taberah said. "We were just about to leave."

Jacob clambered up and followed her quickly through the darkness, both keeping low, ready at any moment to dodge another deadly light. In time Jacob noticed that other figures joined them, and he almost ran from them until he realised that they were also survivors of Taberah's group. While he was comforted by this realisation, he was not comforted by how few of them there were. For a moment he thought that if Whistler had joined them, as he requested, he might have been one of those left behind, turning white light to red.

What kind of world is this, Jacob thought, *where light is dangerous and Hope is an enemy?*

Chapter Six

THE RESISTANCE

The Silver Ghost collected the survivors in the thick of night, and returned them to the Order's headquarters under the blanket of darkness. Jacob could not quite make out how big that command centre was, but it seemed like a single building, masquerading as an abandoned barn.

Taberah immediately convened a meeting, to which Jacob was not invited, much to his chagrin, given how recently he risked death for the Order. He was beginning to think that it was time to move on, but part of him was curious to see what Taberah had up her scarlet sleeves.

He waited outside Taberah's room for what felt like forever. He heard the muffled discussions inside. It seemed that she was consulting with some of her closest advisers, and some of them were warning her not to trust him, and others were supporting her assertion that the Order needed more allies.

Jacob strolled back and forth outside the door, and then he jumped when he turned and found Teller standing there. Teller was a quiet man, who never seemed to walk anywhere, but rather emerged. The gaslight paid no compliments to his features. He was mostly bald, and what few stragglers remained stood on end, as if trying to join their brethren in escaping the prison of his greasy head. Everything about him screamed grease. His face was slimy, and his hands were moist. Even his eyes were greasy in their own way, and he always seemed to give an oily look, as if the very thoughts in his head that those eyes betrayed were also of a greasy nature.

Yet it was perhaps this very element of him that made him so hard to catch, and it seemed that the Regime had made many fruitless attempts, so much so that he joined a handful of others who earned a place on wanted posters throughout the city of Blackout. He was, of course, not at all photogenic, and so he made the perfect example of the Order's degenerate nature in the Regime's perpetual propaganda. Teller kept one of these posters as a trophy on the door of his room in the Order's headquarters. From it he glowered, as if he hated all who looked upon it, and though the paper was so dry that it actually cracked, to any who dared rub their hand against it, Jacob thought that they might immediately be forced to wipe away the grease.

"You came here, I presume, to eavesdrop," Teller said. He drew uncomfortably close to Jacob, as if to eavesdrop on his thoughts.

"No," Jacob stated while taking a step back.

Teller smirked. "Me neither." He fidgeted with his hands, as if they held a bunch of words that he was trying to say. "They are taking you with them, then. To Dustdelving."

"Seems so."

"They say it is a hidden fortress."

"Oh, I—"

"They say it is impossible to find."

"They might say a lot of—"

"No one ever puts it on a map." Teller continued to fidget, as if he was trying to find Dustdelving in his own hands.

"I guess that's wise," Jacob said.

"Yes," Teller replied, with a hint of melancholy. "They never take me."

"Why not?"

"I do not know."

"Have you asked?"

"Yes."

"Well, I'm—"

"We do not get along," Teller interjected. "The leader of the Resistance and I."

"That would explain it then."

"I suppose it would." Teller drew close again, as if he was about to whisper something, perhaps some dark secret of his that Jacob did not want to know, but then they heard the sound of a lock opening on the door, and Teller turned around and scurried away.

Okay, Jacob thought. *I hope the Order aren't all like this.* He was glad that Whistler and Taberah were not. Taberah opened the door and smiled. A rush of people flooded out, nudging and pushing past. Soasa made sure to push the hardest.

Taberah peered down the corridor through which Teller had fled, and she waited until there was no one else around before she spoke.

"I take it that was Teller," she said.

"Right on the first guess," Jacob replied. "Pity there's no money in guessing games."

"He keeps wanting to have a private meeting with me," Taberah explained.

Jacob laughed. "In your quarters, you mean?"

"Probably."

"Not your type?"

"I don't think he's anyone's type, Jacob. He's too—"

"Slimy?"

"That's one word," Taberah said. It seemed she was holding back many others.

"Why do you keep him around?"

"He's useful."

"Like me?" Jacob asked.

"In a different way. He's good at getting information about the Regime, their whereabouts and so forth. I'd just prefer if he stopped looking for private meetings."

"You let me have a private meeting," Jacob pointed out with a grin. "Very private."

"You're different."

"How?"

Taberah paused. "I don't know."

"Sounds dangerous not to know."

"Maybe knowing is just as dangerous," she mused.

"I think the danger is part of what makes it exciting," Jacob said.

"Perhaps. Is that why you became a smuggler?"

"That and the money. You can't spend thrills."

"But you can feel them."

"But the feeling doesn't last."

"So you need another thrill," Taberah said, like the offer of another drink, or another drug.

"You sound like Cala."

"Who's that?"

"An old friend."

"A she?"

"Yes. She liked to take risks all the time. It was all about the thrills."

"I don't take risks on the battlefield," Taberah said, though so far she had proven otherwise.

"What about the bedroom?" Jacob teased.

She tapped her chest in the place where the amulet was. "I don't take risks there either."

Jacob eyed her up and down. "Maybe with me everything's a risk."

"Or maybe you're a safer bet than you think," Taberah said. "Let's go to Dustdelving."

The journey to the stronghold of Dustdelving was a long and winding one, and though there were no windows in Jacob's quarters aboard the Silver Ghost, he could tell that they were climbing a steep mountain and then descending an even steeper valley, all the while twisting and turning, as if the very roads were snakes that slithered across the desert.

"I guess you don't like travel," Whistler said when Jacob almost threw up.

Whistler was out of the rags he wore in the Hold, but his new clothes were not much better. For a start, they were a little too loose, and a little too short. He had grown slightly in height, but shrunk in width. He looked decidedly awkward, but then Jacob mused that he probably did not look much better when he was a teenager. The patchwork on the boy's clothes did not help. The main fabric was a light brown, but the patches were yellow and blue, drawing attention to them. He also wore a brown peaked beret, which did nothing to contain his curls.

"I don't mind travel," Jacob grumbled. "But I tend to drive in a straight line. Easier to reach your destination."

"Easier to spot and kill you," Whistler said. "I thought smugglers would be more cautious."

"Driving like a madman attracts more danger. To smuggle, you have to blend in, become a shadow on the wall, a brick upon the road. They can't notice you or suspect you. Essentially, you have to become one of them."

Whistler looked uncomfortable.

"As far as they're concerned," Jacob added. "It's a ruse."

"They do that too," Whistler said. "They pretend to be us. I don't like ruses."

"I thought that's what your job is all about, to weed out the spies."

"Yes, but it's not one I took willingly, and I like it even less now that I have proven I can fail at it."

"We all make mistakes, Whistler. I failed at mine too."

The Silver Ghost never made a single stop on its journey, not even when the silver glow of the moon was the only light to guide it through the serpentine sands.

"I wish I could look out as we travelled," Jacob said. "I'm tired of seeing silver."

"Taberah doesn't want you to know the way here," Whistler explained.

"With all this twisting and winding, I honestly don't think I'd remember."

"She doesn't want you to know too much," Whistler said, and he seemed doubtful.

"Maybe you shouldn't tell me so much."

"Why? Should I not trust you?"

"It's not that," Jacob said, but a part of him suggested that maybe it was. "Maybe you should not trust everyone else."

Whistler was silent for a time. "I can't live like that," he said. "I hate the doubt, the suspicions."

"In this world that's how we survive," Jacob said.

"But then you shouldn't trust us either," Whistler suggested, as if to expose Jacob's hypocrisy.

"I don't," Jacob stated, and Whistler frowned. "It's been a long time since I trusted anyone."

They stopped suddenly, and Jacob stumbled across the room. He still felt the twisting and turning in his head. Whistler led him out, and handed him a pair of leather goggles. "You'll need these," he said, and he smiled.

Jacob soon knew why, and how the place had earned its name, for there was a ferocious sandstorm that threw every grain of sand into the air, a violent work of weather that assaulted all who stood within it. The sound of the howling wind was horrendous, and it harried every ear as much as the sand would have stung any unprotected eye.

"It's not natural," Whistler said. "I mean, it's manmade. The Resistance uses machinery to kick up the sand, which helps disguise the location."

Jacob tried to respond, but coughed instead as sand lodged in his throat. He shielded his face with his coat and stumbled after Whistler, who kicked up more sand with his boots as he skipped ahead.

They entered a small compound tucked away in the sand, virtually invisible in the dusty haze. Jacob could barely tell who had joined him inside, for his goggles were cased in dust. He removed them to find several people with him, some wearing goggles and large hats, some wearing scarves, and a handful, including Taberah, wearing gas masks. She removed hers now, and she looked as grim without it.

"Hold on," she said.

Suddenly the ground moved, and Jacob grabbed the nearby rail. The platform they were standing upon descended noisily, and Jacob could almost feel the cogs working in his ears.

"Why is it always down we go?" Jacob shouted over the din. "Isn't that where Hell is?" He grinned towards the others, who stared back with sour faces. Only Whistler seemed slightly amused. Taberah looked at Jacob coldly, but did not respond.

The grinding gears stopped, and the platform halted with a jerk. Whistler trotted off, followed by the other members of the Order, many of whom looked noticeably ill-at-ease. Taberah hung behind, and just as Jacob began to depart, she grabbed his arm firmly and held him back.

"You're about to meet the leader of the Resistance," she told him, and she made it sound like an honour that few had been awarded. "Be courteous. Be civil. And Jacob," she added, much more harshly, "leave your jokes behind in the dust or you might become many more grains."

"A little bit of humour goes a long way," Jacob said.

"You're near Hell, remember. You don't want to go any further." Taberah walked off, casting her gas mask to the side, where it clattered off a pile of other masks and face protections, some basic and some ornate. "Throw your mask there," she called back, and perhaps she was not referring to the goggles.

Maybe she has a sense of humour after all, Jacob thought. He followed, but he tucked his goggles into his belt instead. Sometimes there were little victories to be had in the smallest acts of rebellion.

When he caught up with the others, he founded them all standing in a line, as if part of a regiment. If they were an army, they were an undisciplined one, out of uniform. A more convincing soldier, in full military attire, stood across the way, guarding a well-sealed door.

"I've seen better lines on my face," Jacob jested. Taberah shushed him, and Whistler held back a laugh. Taberah glanced at Jacob's belt and then glared at him. He could not help but feel a little proud. There were greater victories when those small acts of rebellion were noticed by the tyrants.

Jacob found waiting outside this door more tiresome than waiting outside Taberah's. He almost wished to be greeted by Teller again, or to sit, or to dance, or to prod the guard to see if he would react. He glanced now and then at Whistler, and the two of them smirked at nothing, and then Jacob feigned his most dignified soldier stance. *Chin up, old boy,* he thought. *The general's watching.* He meant Taberah, but soon he would meet the real general.

The Resistance had protocols in place for meetings like this, many of which Jacob did not like, least of all signing his name on a list. He would rather have just stopped by, had a glass of whiskey, or the bottle if the general was offering, and then given a drunken salute goodbye. He did not see what all the fuss was about, why all the rules and regulations, and why Taberah, of all people, was so keen to follow them.

When the time came for Jacob to enter that mysterious room he stood facing for far too long, only Taberah joined him. Apparently the general was not in the mood for visitors, and Jacob expected no whiskey at all.

Chapter Seven

THE GENERAL

"Meet Edward Rommond," Taberah said, extending her arm towards a man in uniform who stood like a feature in the centre of the perfectly square room.

Jacob was more fascinated by her arm, and the various jewelled bands and bracelets she wore, than the figure she pointed to. When his eyes finally left the tips of her painted fingernails and travelled to where Rommond stood, he was not entirely certain she was introducing anyone at all. The man stood perfectly still, with his hands held behind his back, and at a first glance, and even a second, he could be mistaken for a military statue. Jacob mused that perhaps that it is how he evaded the Regime to date.

"Rommond will do," the man said sternly, breaking the illusion with his bushy moustache, which bobbed up and down as he talked. He had a firm voice, and yet there was a hint of joviality behind it, like perhaps there might have been a hint of a smile behind that masking moustache.

Jacob walked further into the room and offered his hand. Rommond did not immediately take it, but eyed him up and down, as if reading all of his history in his face, all of his deeds and actions in his clothes, and all of his secrets in his eyes. When Jacob felt altogether uncomfortable, as any smuggler did when standing under the spotlight, Rommond seized his hand with both of his and shook it violently.

"Quite the handshake you've got there, old chap," Rommond said, and Jacob raised an eyebrow, thinking the general must have been talking to himself.

"I'm not that old," Jacob replied.

"Evidently," Rommond said, and he eyed Jacob up and down once more. Again Jacob felt uneasy under the spotlight glare of those eyes.

"Jacob," the general said, as if he had seized the name from the vault of Jacob's mind.

"I didn't tell you—"

"I didn't ask you," Rommond interjected. "I asked Tabs before you came in. A good general does everything he can to gain knowledge, of friend or foe."

"Tabs?" Jacob asked, and he could not contain his grin. Taberah looked more than a little embarrassed.

"Maybe one day she'll let you call her that too," Rommond said.

Jacob glanced at Taberah and could not hold back the thought: *Maybe I know her better than you think.*

"Take a seat," the general said, though perhaps it was less of an offer and more of an order.

They complied, *like good little soldiers*, Jacob thought. They sat in the two chairs facing Rommond's desk, while he refused to sit, and so he towered over them like a monument.

Rommond was meticulously dressed, almost as

if he were a toy soldier still in its packaging. His uniform was an almost perfect grey, if there was such a thing, like the exact shade found precisely between black and white, and it was adorned with many medals, all of which were finely polished, and there was not a crease anywhere, nor a stain, nor even a stray hair or particle of dust. "Everything in its place," he was often heard to say. "The pen in the pen rack, the cap on the hat stand, the bullet in the enemy."

"Let's get straight to the point," Rommond said.

"Let's," Jacob said with a smile. Rommond eyed him coldly, as if he could demote ranks with just a glance.

"I've heard you've been busy at Ravenfall," the general continued.

"Ravenfall?" Jacob asked.

"It's code for the Blackout Hope factory," Taberah explained. "And yes, we've scouted their defences."

"Let me guess," Rommond said. "They've got quite a few."

"We've got pictures," Taberah said as she unearthed her notebook and the pictures taken by the dark chamber. She handed them to Rommond.

"Lovely drawings," Rommond said, "but what do you want me to do with them? I've already decorated this room." Jacob looked around and noted the paintings on the walls, all of them from before the time of the Harvest. He also noticed a plaque on the wall behind Rommond's desk, bearing the name *Brooklyn*. This was surrounding by many rifles on display. There were no windows, but there were many gas lamps, generating a dull reddish-yellow hue.

"We need a little help breaking down those defences," Taberah revealed. "We don't have the firepower on our own."

"And you think I have some to spare?" Rommond asked. "A single bullet does not serve two guns."

"Looks like you've got plenty," Jacob said, nodding towards the gun displays.

"If you cared to do your part in this war," Rommond said, "you might have had one."

"I don't know why, there's just something about you that rubs me the wrong way," Jacob shared. He felt he should be a little more giving with his feelings if Rommond would not be more giving with his guns.

Rommond sniffled, and his moustache twitched, as if it too had been rubbed the wrong way. "Perhaps it's the uniform," he suggested.

"I don't have a problem with the military."

"What about authority?" Rommond asked.

"Are you an authority?" Jacob asked in turn.

Rommond did not move, but his eyes fixed on him, like twin barrels of a turret.

"Authority in and of itself is not evil," Rommond said. "It's how the Regime uses it that makes it so."

"And the Resistance?" Jacob quizzed.

Rommond looked at Taberah. "A word," he said, drawing her aside. Jacob could barely make out their hushed conversation, and he could not help but wonder if Rommond was suggesting using those rifles on a certain someone in the room.

From this vantage point Jacob noticed the distinctive emblem of the Resistance in a patch sewn onto the right shoulder of Rommond's uniform. It showed a white equilateral triangle with two lines through it, all upon a royal blue field.

Of the muttered talk Jacob could make out, he heard the following:

"You vouch for him?" Rommond asked, and he eyed Jacob once more, as if to see if his own eyes could vouch for him too.

"I already told you that I do."

"I don't get you sometimes, Tabs."

Taberah smirked. "I don't get you sometimes either. But trust me, Rommond, I have a good feeling about Jacob."

"I trust you, but I'm not so sure about him, or your feelings. I can't load guns with feelings."

They returned soon after, and Jacob forced a smile, as if he was not in any way put out by their secret conversation, and as if he had not heard a word of it.

"So you can spare nothing?" Taberah asked, and she did not sit back down. It seemed she was less willing to stay for tea if the biscuits were not included.

"Regretfully," Rommond said. "If I could, I would."

Jacob was not so sure about that, but it seemed enough to satisfy Taberah.

"Before we go, show us your latest landship," Taberah said, and she sounded as teasing then as she did with Jacob only a few nights before. Rommond did not look so easily seduced, but there was a hint of pride in his eyes, like a child asked to show his favourite toy.

"That," Rommond said, "is something I can

definitely do."

As they left the room, Rommond halted by the door, where a new soldier had taken up watch. Though it was much darker here, with only a single lamp, Rommond seemed to notice something, like a hawk catches sight of his prey.

"Soldier," the general said, turning sharply.

The soldier saluted.

"Where is your number?" Rommond asked.

The soldier panicked, and his lip trembled. He tried to remain still, but he buckled under the glare of Rommond, like a building under a bomb.

Rommond did not give the soldier time to explain. "Do you acknowledge that there is a purpose for every aspect of your uniform?"

"Yes, sir!" the soldier said, with another, more forceful, salute.

"Then do you acknowledge that in not having your number present on said uniform, you are lacking in one or more of these purposes?"

"Yes, sir!"

"Then rectify this lapse, soldier, and do not make it again."

"Yes, sir!"

"Once rectified, consult Field Marshall Magadry and do fifty laps around the yard."

"Yes, sir," the soldier said, but this one was less enthusiastic.

"Dismissed," Rommond said, and it was good enough to be his own salute.

* * *

They followed Rommond down many flights of stairs, into what appeared to be a monumental complex housing a vast arsenal. If the Regime had a factory producing Hope, the Resistance had a factory producing the tools of despair.

"I guess that's a good example," Jacob said as they walked.

"Of what?" Rommond asked.

"Of what rubs me the wrong way."

"Ah," Rommond said. "*Discipline*." He stressed the word, as if it were strong enough to strike any erring soldier. Perhaps, to the ears of Rommond's troops, it was.

"My father was a disciplinarian," Jacob explained. "It didn't exactly stop me from entering the smuggling trade."

"There are two types of discipline," Rommond explained. "Discipline that destroys and discipline that preserves. The Regime is the former. It disciplines through fear and control,

through pain and punishment. To it discipline is not about self-control, but controlling others.

"The Resistance is the latter. We employ discipline to ensure that our goals,

the preservation of our nation, and of the human race, are achieved, with swiftness and success."

"With swiftness and success," Jacob mused. "How's that going for you?"

"Perhaps you would be less mocking if you realised that your success as a smuggler to date has largely depended on manoeuvres we in the Resistance have made."

Jacob scoffed. "If I get to thank you for my successes, can I blame you for my failures too? What manoeuvre did you make that got me arrested?"

Taberah tried to silence Jacob with her eyes, but he paid little attention.

"Maybe that manoeuvre has yet to come," Rommond said.

They passed by many landships on their way to Rommond's latest toy. Some of them were frighteningly big and clunky, while others were little more than converted tractors, and they might have still been tractors had not most of the soil turned to sand after the Harvest.

Soon they came to a landship unlike any of the others. This was a medium-sized vehicle, with smoother edges, a track concealed at the top, and a long turret-mounted gun. It was emerald green, and it had many adornments and embellishments which did not look like they served a function, unless the function was to dazzle the eye, or enchant the heart.

"Pretty," Jacob said. It was perhaps not the word Rommond was hoping for.

"Does it pack a punch?" Taberah asked.

"A knockout," Rommond said, much to Taberah's satisfaction.

"What's it called?" Jacob asked.

"The Hopebreaker." The sound rattled from Rommond's tongue like the fire of the landship's guns, and it left an echo in Jacob's mind, like the ring of a round of turret fire.

"Rather apt," Jacob said.

"It would be more apt if its first field of battle was the Hope factory," Taberah suggested.

"Ah so, now we get to the real reason why you wanted us down here," Rommond said. "Ever the snake, Tabs, winding your way here and there until in range of the bite."

"So says the Desert Hawk," Taberah replied with a smile.

"Perhaps that lets me see further than you."

"Perhaps," she replied, "but I'm the one on the ground, in the sands. The view is different down here."

"It is too early for a direct attack," Rommond said. He walked behind a nearby desk and placed his hands upon it, as if weary from Taberah's insistence. "Our machines are barely ready, and they are too few in number. I need more funding, funding which you cannot offer, and I doubt your enterprising friend can either."

"Not a coil to spare," Jacob said. "Just like your guns."

Rommond ignored him. "When we escalate things, we have to be prepared for them to do the same. That is why I want to be certain that we have everything in place, that we have everything we need. We need perfect timing if we are to win this war."

"I'm not sure there will ever be a perfect time to fight, Rommond. The longer we leave them to their own devices, the more devices they will have to use against us."

"You know where my mind is on this, Taberah,"

Rommond said, and Jacob noticed the use of her full name now, as if they were no longer acquainted. "My plans have been drawn up for some time, and they will not be redrawn overnight. I cannot reveal my arsenal this soon."

"Rommond, we need your firepower *now*, not later."

Rommond placed his gun upon the table like a writer places an exclamation point at the end of a sentence. There was a hint of finality about the gesture, like an announcement that this was the end of the debate. Taberah must have recognised it, for she did not sustain her verbal assault. She turned and left, and if silence was her shield, it was also her weapon, leaving a sting behind in the quiet air.

"Dismissed," Rommond said, looking at Jacob sternly as if he were a soldier on duty. Jacob did not like the idea that perhaps he was, that somehow he had been smuggled into a war he had no interest in fighting. Rommond kept his gaze until Jacob buckled like an iron chamber under a bunker buster. He left the room, and as soon as he did he was dragged aside by Taberah.

"He will help," she said, "but not as much as I would have liked."

"It didn't look like he was going to help at all."

"He won't field the Hopebreaker—that's as much his baby as Brooklyn was—but if we can get him more funds he might let us use some of his older models. They're nothing more than tin cans now, but they're better than what we've got."

"Your Silver Ghost looked mean enough."

"Looks, sure," she said. "That's a transport vehicle. It isn't really designed for fighting."

"Could've fooled me."

"Good," she said. "I hope it fools everyone."

Jacob paused for a bit. "Who or what is Brooklyn?"

Taberah looked away, and for the first time since they had met, Jacob caught a hint of sadness in her eyes. "It would be unfair of me to say, especially so close to Rommond's room. And it is too sad a tale to tell. Indeed, to Rommond, and even to me, it is the real hope breaker."

Jacob did not ask any more about it, but he felt a hint of the sorrow that Taberah clearly felt, and perhaps if he could see deep into the souls of others like Rommond seemed to be able to, he would have seen the sorrow that dwelt in the bunker of Rommond's heart.

Chapter Eight

PATRONAGE

Taberah arranged for their departure from Dust-delving that evening. It seemed that if Rommond would not supply landships in the morning, it was not worth her while staying the night. Rommond did not appear in any way slighted by this, as if he was well used to how she behaved.

"So where are we off to now?" Jacob asked.

"Blackout," Taberah replied.

"My smuggling haunt," Jacob said. "Maybe I can smuggle you in."

"I'll get in fine on my own, Jacob. And out. It's what we'll be bringing out that might take a little bit more effort."

"Oh? What's that?"

"Money."

"You've got my attention." She really did.

"The Baroness of Blackout owes me a favour or two," Taberah explained. "I got her some amulets back in the day, saved her some hassle."

"Then why not just call in those favours?"

"Because with her it doesn't work like that."

"How does it work then?" Jacob asked.

"Well, she's a bit of a romantic."

Jacob shrugged. "So send her a card with a poem on one side and asking for money on the other."

Taberah laughed. "There's little doubt that you're a smuggler."

"I'm not so sure," Jacob said. "It looks like I work for the Order now."

"We may need your smuggling skills yet," Taberah said. "I'll need you to do a little pretending first. Do this job well and we'll all be very grateful."

"What is it Rommond said about not loading guns with feelings?" Jacob asked. "I can't feed myself with gratitude."

"Last I looked, you were eating my food."

"A man's got to eat."

"Jacob, smuggling is what you're all about. Don't give up just when you've become useful."

"I'm not giving up. I just want to know what I get in return. I've already done the best part of a week's work for the Order, without a single coil to my name."

"Some of us don't work for money," Taberah said. "But if you still feel you need compensation, then take ten percent of what the Baroness is sending."

"Ten percent doesn't sound like much."

"When you see how much one hundred percent is, you'll change your mind."

"What if I don't?"

"You will," Taberah stated. "The question is, will you change your mind about taking a cut?"

"I don't think so."

"I have faith in you."

Jacob scoffed. "Faith isn't worth a single coil."

* * *

As the Silver Ghost wormed its way through the sands from Dustdelving to Blackout, Jacob was briefed on the plan to impress the maudlin Baroness by pretending to be courting Taberah, as well as his expected behaviour in the presence of that illustrious lady. *Etiquette* was the word of the day, and it was not a word Jacob was particularly fond of.

Whistler soon became one of Jacob's unofficial mentors when Taberah and several other Order members gave up in frustration. It was not that Jacob could not learn. He did not want to, and he quite enjoyed doing everything they told him not to. Had they told him to dispense with formality, he might have been more formal just to annoy them.

They had left behind the winding paths from Dustdelving, where Jacob was again refused access to a window, and Whistler turned every idle opportunity into a lesson. On one such occasion he ran around the vehicle with great excitement. When he returned, he unfurled a silk cloth to reveal a series of silver utensils.

"This one is for dessert," he said eagerly, barely taking a breath before moving on to the next. "And this one is for tea. And this one is for soup. And this one is for gravy. And this one is if you let the other one fall. And this one—"

"Okay!" Jacob said. "I think I'll be fine."

"No," Whistler replied. "No, you don't get how important this is." Perhaps he meant that it was important to him, because Jacob could not see why anyone would be so obsessed with what spoon to use for what. He had used a spoon to shove inside a gear box to get his vehicle moving, and he was sure it was not designed for that purpose.

"I get it," Jacob said. "I'll be fine."

Whistler hung his head, and the spoons all mixed together, as if they no longer felt separated by purpose and rank.

"All right then, tell me what this one's for," Jacob said, picking up what looked like any other spoon.

"That's for jam," Whistler said, beaming.

"What if I don't have jam?"

"Then don't use it."

Hell, Jacob thought. *I'll never remember this stuff.*

And so Whistler carried on with his cataloguing of the various utensils that Jacob was expected to know, and their singular and most sacred use. Jacob thought the kid needed new toys.

What a great hobby the rich have, Jacob thought, *worrying about such pointless things.*

When they came close to Blackout, Taberah and Jacob departed on their own, and the Silver Ghost faded away into the sandy haze. Taberah led them to one of the smaller entrances, where fewer guards were posted, but Jacob urged her to try his route instead.

"Trust me," he said. "You don't pick the door with few guards. You pick the door with none."

He led them into the shadows that clung to the city walls.

"If I ruled the Regime, I'd have guards on every door," Taberah said.

"Thankfully, you don't rule the Regime then."

They passed by small groups of people, who clung to the shadows. Many of them averted their gaze, and some of them pulled up their hoods or turned away to hide their faces. A few made quick exchanges, and they were so quick, and it was so dark, that it was impossible to tell what was traded. Maybe it was guns, or maybe it was drugs, or maybe it was amulets. In the shadows there was nothing that could not change hands.

"Friends of yours?" Taberah whispered when they passed from earshot.

"I don't have friends," Jacob said.

"Just opportunities for profit?" she quizzed.

"I prefer the word *clients*. But no, I have nothing to do with these. You shouldn't either."

They continued through the black market that reinforced the outer walls, keeping their heads low and their pace fast. Some seemed to recognise Jacob and gave him a subtle nod, but no one gave a nod to Taberah; they gave her a cautious glare instead.

"Here we are," Jacob announced as they came upon a small crevice in the wall, just large enough to squeeze through.

"So you're proving useful after all."

"I told you I would be."

"And now I believe you."

"You didn't before?"

"I believed in Whistler's endorsement of you."

"You put a lot of stock in his assessment," Jacob noted.

"Yes," she said.

79

"I hope you don't mind me asking, but is he your kid?"

"Yes."

"You don't exactly look like the mothering type."

"I suppose not."

"Sore topic?" Jacob quizzed.

"Let's just keep moving."

The passage Jacob led them through was extremely narrow, and full of moss, and it might have been full of cobwebs were it not frequented so much. Jacob told Taberah that the criminal underworld of Blackout had many of these discrete entrances, and some were designated as exits, and anyone caught using the wrong one might have wished they had been caught by the Regime instead.

In time they came into the backstreets of Blackout, and from there Jacob handed the reins over to Taberah, who led them to the home of the Baroness.

As they entered, Taberah reminded Jacob of the training he had received, of how he was to behave, of how they would pretend to be deeply in love. Taberah lashed him with that dreaded word *etiquette*, like a rider might whip a horse. Jacob took on the air of a gentleman, and as he linked her arm, he thought he seemed quite dignified indeed.

Baroness Ebronah was an old lady, old in age and old in custom, and both were clear at a glance. Her hair had gone from black to grey, and now it was going from grey to white, as if she was surpassing her elderly years and being consumed by the light that began all things. She wore a dated dress from the time before the Regime came into a power, a faded rose-coloured gathering of many lace-trimmed skirts upon a crinoline frame, which restricted her movement, but formed around her like a throne. She wore a single white arm-length glove, which might itself have started black, and then grey. She did not wear a hat, unlike many others of her generation, but there were many large and ornate headpieces upon the furthest wall, replacing what might have been even larger and more ornate paintings, all of which were outlawed by the Regime.

She turned to them slowly, and Jacob was struck by the sharpness of her features, which stood out most at odds with the roundness of her dress. Her nose was pointed, her chin was pointed, and her cheeks were pointed. Even her words were angular, her tone sharp, so much so that all ears were cut by them.

"Do come in," she said, but these words of welcome almost sounded like a scolding, as if they had arrived unannounced, and would leave unappeased.

They complied, arm in arm, which she must have noticed, for her frown softened just a little, and beneath the wrinkles Jacob thought he could see just the hint of a smile, albeit a pointed one.

"Do sit down," she said, and the scolding was softer.

Jacob led Taberah to a mahogany sofa, adorned with cream-coloured cushions, just a little faded, like everything else in the room. Taberah gathered her dress up awkwardly and sat down. Jacob decided to wait until she was fully seated before joining her. Ebronah must have noticed this little act of chivalry, for her smile deepened.

"Your latest conquest?" the Baroness asked Taberah.

"My lovely consort," Taberah corrected. "Jacob."

"How do you do," Jacob said. He held back a laugh.

Ebronah studied him a bit like Rommond did. Jacob noticed that when it came to being part of the Resistance, suspicion was a way of life.

"We wanted to pay you a little visit," Taberah said. "It has been too long."

"Money," Ebronah said sternly. "You want money."

Taberah was taken aback and stuttered her response. "I … oh … well … we wouldn't—"

"We all want money," Jacob interjected. "It's the way of the world."

"Not this world," Ebronah said. "Some want Hope instead."

"And money can buy it," Jacob suggested.

"Or destroy it," Taberah added.

This raised an eyebrow from Ebronah. "Oh? Do tell."

"I cannot say much," Taberah explained, "only that our plan may starve the Regime out of power and restore things to the way they were."

Ebronah looked silently into the mirror. Perhaps she pondered how she looked back then, how her painting-covered walls looked, how all of Altadas looked. Perhaps she saw in that mirror a reflection not just of her own life, but of her husband's, and their life together.

"We need funding," Taberah said.

"Did Rommond send you?"

"No, but this money is for him."

"He never comes here any more."

"It's too risky," Taberah said.

"It's risky for you too. He used to take those risks."

"Not since Brooklyn."

Ebronah was silent again for a time. The mirror stole her gaze once more. Perhaps in it she saw Rommond in his younger days. Perhaps in it she saw Brooklyn too.

"I'm in a generous mood," the Baroness said.

"Is that a yes?" Taberah asked.

"Yes," Ebronah said. "I will have Samith prepare ten thousand coils for you."

Taberah's eyes widened, and Jacob was almost certain that his did too.

"That's too much," Taberah said, and Jacob hoped her comment was pure politeness. There was no such thing as too much.

"Too much to carry in your purse," Ebronah said. "How will you get it out of Blackout? You usually have smugglers bring valuable things in, not out."

"Jacob is an expert smuggler. He will make sure we get it out of the city and down to Dustdelving."

Jacob almost scoffed at this involuntary assignment, but he feigned an eager smile instead. "Happy to help the cause," he said. He would rather help himself to the crates of coils instead.

"Just to be clear," Taberah said. "This is a gift, not

a loan, correct?"

The Baroness smiled like a banker. "A gift. Consider yourself free of the Treasury for this amount. I'll include a waiver with my seal on it, just in case you run into trouble."

"Thank you. That puts my mind at ease."

They stayed for tea, and they had some light conversation, and Jacob held Taberah's hand delicately. He was only forced to use one spoon to stir his tea, and he had little trouble with the game of pleasantries, which he indulged as, he reassured himself, a form of mocking.

When they were finished, Taberah curtsied and Jacob bowed, and it was all very prim and proper, and they waited outside for Samith to meet them with their patron's endowment.

"Why did you ask her if it was a gift?" Jacob whispered. "Surely she wouldn't want the money back if she's supporting the Resistance."

"It doesn't work like that," Taberah explained. "The Treasury rarely gives money away for nothing. Usually there's a price. Often there is interest. Sometimes people pay with their lives. Trust me, you don't want the Treasury's debt collectors after you. They are ruthless when it comes to ensuring payment in full."

"I'm glad my ten percent is not a loan then. It doesn't exactly sound like they're on our side."

"The Treasury is a neutral party. It supports no one but its own financial interests. It is a purely money-driven endeavour."

"Sounds lovely," Jacob said with a smile. "Maybe I'll join."

Taberah scoffed. "You're either born into it or you're not. Consider it the vestiges of an ancient royalty, back before the time of the Regime."

"Surely they can't be that neutral then if the Regime ousted them from power."

"Money is its own kind of power, Jacob." Jacob knew that well. "There are many in the Treasury who support our efforts," Taberah continued, "but few of them are as open or as giving as Baroness Ebronah. The best most of them will offer is a long-term loan, and Rommond has too many of them hanging over his head. He makes many amazing machines of war, but war itself is a machine oiled by money, and our funds are growing very thin."

In the end Samith never met with them at all, but the Baroness greeted them for a final farewell. Jacob straightened up as soon as she came into view.

"Quickly now," the Baroness said. "The current guard has been paid to have an hour's nap. You will not get any more time than that, so use it wisely. I trust you have a suitable vehicle."

"I've arranged a delivery truck," Taberah said.

"Good. I'll see that it is loaded up. Goodbye, Taberah, and send my regards to Rommond. Tell him that I can only keep the Grand Treasurer away for so long."

"I will," Taberah said, and she looked suddenly grim, as if she had been told the most harrowing news.

"Right then," Jacob said, clapping his hands together loudly. "Time for one more smuggling job. Let's hope it goes smoothly." Though he felt more than a little excited, a large part of him told him that the job ahead would be a bumpy, and perhaps a deadly, one.

Chapter Nine

THE SMUGGLER'S ART

The crates were loaded into the delivery truck quickly by men who looked as though they had been paid to look at everything but what they were packing, and anyone but whom they were packing for. Their tightly clenched lips looked as though they had been sealed with gold, perhaps the Treasury's own kind of sacrament of silence.

The truck itself was just large enough to fit all ten crates, with a seat for a driver and passenger at the front. It looked old and worn, and its many cogs and levers needed to be oiled considerably before Jacob climbed inside. A small clock dial ticked away noisily inside, forcibly reminding them of the fading minutes of that one-hour window of opportunity.

"You might want to hide in the back," Jacob said to Taberah, and he reached into the back to make some room. "They usually expect just one driver."

"I'm not going with you."

"Why not?"

"I can't risk getting captured."

"That isn't very reassuring."

"Then don't get caught," Taberah said, and she slammed the door shut.

The truth was that he was more relieved than he let on. He preferred to work alone, where his success or failure rested solely on his own merit. He did not like to rely on others, and he was not entirely convinced that Taberah was reliable. From the worry that was evident in her expression, it seemed that she was not convinced that he was either. He felt almost compelled to prove her wrong.

The steam truck was agonisingly slow to start up, no matter how much coal he shovelled into the furnace, nor how much steam the smokestack spewed. He had driven these vehicles before, however, and he knew that they took a while to heat up, but once they were going they could move at incredible speeds, and were often harder to stop than they were to start. He glanced back at the tightly-sealed crates when he had no more levers left to pull, when the truck chugged along at a steady slow pace through the dark streets of Blackout. There was something reassuring about his cargo, something he felt he needed in the very unsettling city his truck noisily crept through.

The first barrier was an unmanned checkpoint, which he knew for certain should have a full contingent of guards. It seemed that the Baroness had paid for a lot of naps this watchless night.

The second barrier had one guard on duty, who simply motioned him through without a second glance. In fact, it seemed that he was not looking at the truck at all, but at a newspaper that bore the headline: *The Regime quashes terrorist menace. Rommond killed.* Jacob had seen such headlines before, even one about

Taberah's supposed assassination. None of it was true. Yet he hoped it was not a kind of premonition. He hoped even more that tomorrow's paper would not speak of how a precious cargo meant for the Resistance had been stopped, and the driver killed.

He felt the steam truck begin to pick up a little speed, and he had to slow it down, to avoid waking any napping guards. These vehicles could be temperamental beasts. *Steady, girl,* he thought. He patted the dashboard, as if to calm her down.

His heart sank when he saw the third checkpoint. A figure stood there facing him, blocking the way. He had a second of internal debate: *Stop or full throttle?* He knew he could easily run over the guard, but there were several more checkpoints to go, and he did not think the blood of the Regime was a good colour for a truck he hoped to keep unsearched. He decided to stop, to play this one tactfully. Sometimes tact was the deadliest weapon.

The truck ground to a halt, and the coil-filled crates slid across the back noisily, as if they were prisoners calling out for help to the nearby guard. The furnace begged for more of its own precious cargo, but Jacob refused to feed it. He clutched the handle of the shovel tightly as he watched the silhouette outside move around to the side of the vehicle. Sometimes a real weapon was better. *One strike and he's out,* he thought. *Another demon down. No one will miss him.*

The door opened suddenly, and Jacob flinched, but he flinched even more when he saw who got in: a familiar face from a long time ago.

"Long time, no see," the woman said, and she

spat a piece of gum onto the windscreen. "If you can still see where you're going, that is," she added, and she giggled, but the hoarseness of her voice made it anything but endearing.

"Cala," Jacob said, mostly from amazement.

"That's my name," she replied. "Better if you don't use it here though." She paused and turned to him. "Well? Are you going to drive or what?"

"Oh, right." Jacob shovelled some coal into the furnace and cranked the engine lever. Though it was noisy, he could still hear Cala chewing gum beside him, and could still hear her voice cranking levers in his brain. *Not quite a demon*, he thought. *Not quite.*

He glanced at her as the steam truck jerked forward. She wore tight leather trousers and a matching coat, both browner from oil stains than they were when she got them first. The buttons were oversized, and she wore two belts, more for show than anything else. A pair of goggles perched in her dishevelled hair, but Jacob knew that they were not for show; she liked to get her hands dirty, but she liked to keep her eyes clean. Her eyes were her strongest feature, with a deep and mesmerising blue, surrounded by thick black eyeliner. Perhaps they would have been brown too were it not for those goggles.

"How long's it been?" she asked, stretching her legs out until her black boots rested against the windscreen.

"Do you have to do that?" Jacob asked her.

"Do what? This?" She pressed her feet against the window harder, until Jacob thought that it might crack at any moment. "Hell, Jake. Lighten up. It's not even yours."

"All the more reason not to wreck it," he said.

She placed her feet back on the ground and clambered over to him, where she whispered in his ear, "I remember that you liked to wreck a lot of things."

"Yeah, well that was years ago," he said, pushing her away.

"You were a smuggler than, and you're a smuggler now. Doesn't look like much has changed."

"Well, it has."

"If you say so," Cala said. "So, how's life been keeping you?"

"Fine," Jacob said irritably. There was an awkward pause as Jacob concentrated on the road ahead, despite Cala regularly ruining his concentration by crossing and uncrossing her legs. The leather purred as she moved.

Cala turned to him with a pout. "Aren't you going to ask how I've been doing?"

"No," Jacob said.

"I'll tell you anyway. I've been doing better since we split, or since *you* split. Got in with a new crowd. Much better than our old lot. Big plans. Lots to do."

"Good," Jacob said. "Keep you busy. Keep you out of trouble."

"Busy, yes," Cala said. "But out of trouble? Nah. If trouble was a city, I'd go there. That's where all the fun is."

Jacob could not entirely deny it, but he would not admit that to Cala, not after everything he had been through with her. Too much trouble sapped the fun out of it, and she was always too much trouble. Even now.

"How did you find me?" Jacob asked.

"Oh, you know me," Cala said. "I'm good at finding things. 'Specially people."

Jacob wished it was not true. He had smuggled people in and out of many cities with Cala's help. Yet he could not quite smuggle himself out of her all-pervading view.

"So, Jacob, what are you smuggling this time?" she asked. She stretched back and banged her fist on one of the crates.

"Don't go near them," Jacob reprimanded.

"What, is it dangerous? Will we explode if I open one of them?" She seemed like she might just try, for the fun of it.

"Cala, can you just do what I say? Just leave them alone and let me do my job."

"I'll leave 'em alone if you tell me what your job is."

"Why are you so curious?"

"When have I never been? There's no box I wouldn't open."

Jacob knew that well enough. He still had a large burn upon his upper right arm from some of her careless explorations. He was not exactly extra careful back then either, and he was lucky he did not have many more scars.

Cala cocked her head as she waited for Jacob's response.

"It's coils, just coils," Jacob explained.

"How much?"

"10k."

"Nice."

"It'd be nicer if they were all mine."

"How much is your cut?"

"1k."

"Not bad," she said, and she paused. "Why don't you make off with the lot?"

The thought had crossed Jacob's mind. He had the getaway vehicle. If he could escape from the clutches of the Regime, perhaps he could escape from the clutches of the Resistance too, and live out a very comfortable life in a remote town. Hell, he could build his own town with that kind of money. Jacobville had a certain ring to it.

"I don't go back on my word," Jacob stated. "I said I'd smuggle this out."

"Who's it for?"

"I'd rather not say."

"Now that just makes me *have* to know."

Jacob shook his head in despair. He knew she would keep prodding. "The Resistance."

"You always did go in for them, didn't you?"

"What do you mean?"

"Well, it was all about the amulets at one stage. Always trying to topple the Regime."

"I don't care about the Regime."

"Sure you do. We all do. Especially if we're on the outside."

"I'm just doing it for the money."

"Whatever you say, Jake."

"What are you doing here anyway?" Jacob asked

her. "I thought you headed up north."

"I did. I just came back for a little … top-up." She pulled a large bag of white powder out of her coat and dangled it before him. It bore the familiar symbol of a swallow perched upon a large letter H, the emblem of the powerful drug Hope.

"Bloody hell, Cala, we're supposed to be destroying this stuff, not keeping it."

She grinned. "Where are we going again?"

"Hell," he said, rolling his eyes.

"Never been there. Is that a place?"

"I shouldn't have let you in," Jacob said, shaking his head.

"You didn't. I let myself in."

"I should have stopped you."

Cala laughed. "When have you ever been able to do that?"

He rolled his eyes again. "Just stop distracting me and let me do my job."

"Look, Jake, we're all just trying to scratch out a living here. You do your amulet crap and I do my bit. People *want* what I've got, Jacob." She took a bit on her finger and rubbed it on her tongue.

"Hell, Cala, you're taking it as well?"

"It's just a little taste," she replied, and she sniffed a line of the powder up and blinked rapidly, as if somehow her eyes were processing too much visual information. "Gotta know how good it is. It's part and parcel of business." She paused and turned to him. "You want some?"

"Of course I don't want some!" he snapped.

"We used to be like *that*," she said, crossing her

fingers as if to remind him of their intertwined limbs. She banged her boots on the dashboard in frustration. The truck groaned in response.

"Well, that's over," Jacob replied. "And if it wasn't over then, it would be now that I know you're dealing Hope."

"Lighten up, Jake. The world could do with a little Hope."

They ignored each other for a little while, Cala looking out the side window as a rain began to fall, Jacob glaring out the front window at the dim road ahead. From here he could see the final two checkpoints for leaving Blackout.

The first was another abandoned checkpoint. Cala pulled one of the brake levers, and the steam truck stuttered forward until Jacob pulled the others. It slowly creaked to a halt.

"This is me," she said.

About time, Jacob thought. Yet he did not like stopping here. He glanced at the clock dial, with all its taunting seconds passing by. Then suddenly Cala grabbed him by the collar and kissed him intensely. He was so taken aback he did not think to push her away.

"Give me a shout, Jake," she said, handing him a card with her number on it. The back had the symbol of a yellow fist upon a mushroom cloud. Jacob has never seen this symbol before, but it seemed very appropriate for Cala.

"You know they monitor all calls now," he said.

"I know," she said, and she grinned at him. "But maybe you're not worth monitoring."

"You seem to think otherwise."

"Maybe we're more interesting together."

She kicked the door open and hopped outside. "Thanks for the ride," she said with a smile. "Let me know if I can return the favour." She placed her goggles on as the rain splattered on her head. "Gotta keep the eyes clean," she said, as if she knew that this might annoy him.

"Goodbye," Jacob said.

"See you around," she replied. Jacob hoped not.

He sighed deeply when she slammed the door and sauntered away, stumbling a little as she went. She patted her coat pocket where she had stuffed the bag of Hope, and she nodded to herself in reassurance. Jacob glanced at her seat and the floor below it to make sure she had not left anything behind. He did not want to give her any excuse to return.

He looked back to the road and got the truck moving again. It was even more sluggish than before. He shovelled more coal into the furnace. There was only one more checkpoint to go. He was so close. This was what hope really was. He fed the furnace another meal. The smoke and steam almost began to thicken, fogging up the windscreen. Through the dimness he could see the final checkpoint up ahead. It was so close now. He was on the edge of freedom. He threw more coal in, until the flames lapped at his legs, hungry for more. He could feel the truck speeding up, but his view was growing more and more obscured. He stretched forward to wipe the windscreen, and then he felt a sudden jerk, and heard a loud crash, and he began to see bits of a broken barrier upon the bonnet.

Damn, he thought. He dared not speak it, in case someone or something else might hear.

But then he heard other sounds, the noises of machines gearing up. He tried to see out, but the windows were still badly steamed. Suddenly the dimness of the road up ahead lit up, and he realised in horror that a spotlight had been turned on. He swerved to avoid it, but others followed. Then he felt the ground behind him quake, and though he could not see them, he knew that the Regime's war machines were in pursuit.

Chapter Ten

THE DEVIL'S MARCH

Jacob cranked levers and adjusted gears, and he fed the fires of the furnace until he began to sweat from heat as well as fear. The steam truck stormed out of Blackout's reach and into the emptiness of the desert all around, where no spotlights lived, and where no spotlights were needed to see him belting across the sandy expanse.

He was so preoccupied with gaining speed that he did not have time to glance back at what was following, but he knew they followed, because the ground continued to quake behind him. When at last he had reached the peak of the vehicle's acceleration, he cast an eye on his assailants: two giant walking machines, with four large steel legs supporting a cubical structure with crenellations, like a castle tower that could no longer stand beside its walls. Within this structure were several Regime soldiers, and upon it summit one of them stood and pointed, and aimed his gun at his elusive target. This strange four-legged creature would have sank into the sand were it not for the speed at which those well-oiled legs moved, and though they were not designed for the desert, it seemed that the desert could not stop the roaming fortifications.

They pursued him far into the golden wastes, where every direction taunted its endless rolling dunes, and they pursued him long into the night, until the very night itself began to roll away, replaced by the emerging sun with its many emerging rays.

He began to hear gunfire behind him, and he saw here and there little pockets of leaping sand where the bullets missed his truck. He began to worm his way through the sand, twisting and turning like a snake, and the bullets continued to rattle down periodically. He was glad that the Regime was conservative with its firing, and that these Moving Castles only had so much supplies, but he knew that they really only needed a single well-aimed bullet to bring the whole chase to a close, and his life to an end.

He was concentrating so much on speed and swerving that he began to lose track of his actual bearings. He cast an eye on the compass that was made into the dashboard, but its needle was erratic, flickering between west and north-west. The desert had few signposts, and few had mapped these parts, and fewer still had wandered through the emptiness and the heat and wandered back again.

In time he saw something ahead that was not the natural formations of dunes, and he wondered if it was a mirage, a little haven from the chase summoned by his pleading mind and delivered to his all too eager eyes. He saw a large wooden sign marking the entrance into a more rocky part of the desert, surrounded here and there by little strips of barbed wire, much of which was now buried by the mounting tides of sand. When Jacob was close enough to read the sign, he had a second of debate: it read *Warning! The Devil's March*, and he was not sure he had the Devil's permission to enter this unholy land.

But there was no time to choose, and no time to change his mind. He could only shovel another pile of coal into the fires, like a sacrificial offering, and hope all the while that he would not have to sacrifice himself as well.

Jacob stopped for nothing or no one. Acceleration was his ally, speed his friend. Even though he now drove across the Devil's territory, the Devil could not stop him now.

A sea of sand was before him, punctuated here and there by large rocky mounds, like the bony ridges of a god's spine buried deep beneath the sand. These dusty slopes were everywhere, and they were so monstrous in size that Jacob knew it would be impossible to drive up or over any of them.

The land was not the only new enemy. The dawning sun was oppressing, hanging low to blind any who dared enter this land, or perhaps to warn them to turn back. The glare filled the cockpit like a passenger, until every piece of metal, every crag and cog, was illuminated, until the very metal itself glared back, and might have blinded whatever eyes the sun had. Jacob was glad to have his goggles then, for he quickly slipped them on, and they dulled the unbearable light.

The Moving Castles bounded after him, and if he had not glanced in his mirrors to see them, he would have still known that they were there, for the ground shook beneath them, and his truck shook in sympathy—or perhaps in fear.

Jacob saw what looked like a thin wisp of smoke up ahead, and he breathed an audible sigh of relief, for he thought it must be from a nearby town, and so he could soon be out of the Devil's March. He was wrong.

He drove towards it at great speed, the wheels of the truck kicking up sand that was then kicked even higher by the metal feet of the Moving Castles behind him. He squinted his eyes to see better, and to see farther, and he realised that the wisp of smoke was instead a winding pillar of sand.

He swerved to the right just in time, but even as he did, and the truck drifted from its own momentum, he felt it drift even further, tugged by the great winds that had thrown the sand into such a vertical fury. He revved and changed gears, and he grimaced at the sound of cogs and latches screeching into place. From this vantage point, as he feverishly and fervently grabbed and pulled at all controls in sight, he could see the Moving Castles coming dangerously close, drawing in for their checkmate.

The truck rocked upon the sand, the wheels spun, and the sand sprang away like tiny fleeing citizens. Jacob heard the crates in the back sliding back and forth, and clanging off the sides. Then just as a great iron foot clashed down only metres away, the truck leapt forward, and Jacob was almost thrown from his seat from the force.

A hail of bullets pelted off the truck, and Jacob

ducked instinctively. He saw dents and holes in the bonnet, and when he glanced back he saw many more perforations in the casing of the truck, letting light in to reveal his precious cargo. One of the crates was also hit, and the holes revealed another kind of light, the dull glimmer of the coils inside, the idols of the Treasury, and borrowed idols for everybody else.

He heard the crates clang off the back doors, and he grimaced, but then he heard an even more unpleasant noise: the sound of one of the door's latches becoming loose. He looked back quickly and saw that one of the back doors was open slightly, but that the latch was still partly, precariously, in place. He also saw that several of the crates were leaning against that door, against that latch, as if trying to escape their prison, as if trying to unite their own iron sheen with the golden sands of the desert.

Jacob's mind cranked away as quickly as the truck. He could continue his hurried flight, eventually throwing off his chasers, but the more he sped, and the more the rocky land threw his cargo back and forth, the more chance he had of losing it. He could get out with his life, perhaps, but as a smuggler that was not enough.

He slammed on the breaks and braced himself. The crates slid towards the cockpit and struck the back of his chair like prisoners attacking their captor, eliciting an audible grunt and an even more audible groan from him. He took a deep breath and bit his lip to numb the pain, then he turned the truck sharply to the left, and the crates slid in the opposite direction. When he drove forward again they slammed towards the right back door, which was still fully sealed.

This action helped close the gap for his chasers, and they were almost upon him once more. He heard the rattle of gunfire, and he ducked just in time as the window to his right smashed to pieces, and as bullets riddled the inside of the truck. One of them smashed the glass of the compass and knocked the needle to the floor. *No worries*, he thought. It was not helping him anyway.

A dust devil sprang up just before him, between two rocky ridges, like a sentinel blocking a gate. He turned and passed between more sandy mounds, but more dust devils sprang up, as if they were sleeping guardians woken by the sound of iron and steel.

Jacob navigated between these, and he felt their awful pull, and he grimaced as sand blew through one broken window, past his irritated nose, and out the other window into the maw of the spinning spirit of the sand. Perhaps those broken windows helped him, for it meant the air blew through instead of blowing the entire truck into those sandy jaws.

One of the Moving Castles was not so lucky, for a dust devil sprang upon it as if it did not like the spirit of machines. The man upon the crenellations was sucked into the whorl with a scream, and the metal legs ground to a halt as the bashing breeze and lashing winds held it in place. Then the legs began to sink into the sand, as much a meal for the ground as it was the air. It sank until it was just a metal tower. It was a Moving Castle no more.

Jacob had little time to gloat or celebrate, however, for the other machine monster still bounded after him, and the man aboard it began to fire more rapidly and more chaotically. Jacob was afraid less that he would be hit by the Regime's perfect aim, but by some random throw of the die, a random hit to some random part of his heart. He did not care much for a random grave in the desert.

There were many devils in this hellish waste, springing up and spinning around, and some of them battled with each other, until one consumed the other and became a large twisting spectre of the sand. Some sat in a single spot like regal figures, and others shot across the land with ferocious speeds, as if they were the knights of some ancient elemental kingdom.

The furnace gulped down another meal, and it begged for more, but Jacob gulped in turn when he saw that there was little left to feed it. The coal supply was running low. Without the element of fire, and its daughter steam, Jacob's own kingdom would come to a sudden end.

Up ahead he saw a line of figures surrounded by vehicles. From this vantage point they were mere silhouettes, but even from here he could see what looked like shoulder-mounted rocket pads. He did not need to speculate for long, for a shrieking rocket sailed dangerously past him, exploding into a large dune and raining down to create several more little dunes. He swerved as another rocket roared past, and he began to wonder if this was actually the Regime ahead, armed like the Resistance to lure him into a trap called death.

The Moving Castle kept up its pursuit, and it dodged the rockets just as easily as Jacob did. There was one thing that could be said about the Regime: its forces were persistent. They would chase their prey into the mouth of death, and perhaps there they would continue to chase its soul.

The figures up ahead began to grow more apparent, and Jacob thought he saw what looked like Taberah's warwagon, but he could not quite make out if she stood among those rocket-firing people. Then he saw that some of them were holding up large square pieces of mirror, and they were reflecting the sunlight at the eyes of those in the Moving Castle.

Another rocket sprang past, and Jacob swerved, but this time the Moving Castle could not evade it in time. The tower exploded, and the legs collapsed, and bits and pieces of the machine struck the side of Jacob's truck, and they, combined with the force of the wind and the explosion, almost toppled it to its side.

Jacob continued to drive towards the figures up ahead, even though it looked as though they were rearming and aiming new rockets at him. He glanced at the solitary lump of coal in the coal chamber beside him, and at the fading flames of the furnace, desperately reaching out to taste that final piece. He knew that even if those people ahead were not the Resistance, he would have to surrender to them, for without fire he could not begin another flight.

Chapter Eleven

TREASURE

Jacob shoved on the door, and it collapsed outwards into the sand. He almost collapsed out after it, but he stumbled to his feet and shielded his eyes from the still sizzling sun. Taberah stood over him with her own intense glare.

"Well, I did it," Jacob said.

"Just about," Taberah replied. She knocked on the bonnet of the truck, which was crinkled and buckled as if a giant had knocked on it before.

"10,000 coils," Jacob said.

"And a good hundred coils damage to this truck."

"A minor inconvenience," Jacob said, gritting his teeth. His own inconvenience had not been so minor. It almost cost him his life.

"It's lucky we were here," Taberah said.

"I'm not sure you've brought me any luck since I've met you," Jacob grumbled. "And besides, you could have met me further into the Devil's March. Maybe more of the steam truck would have survived then."

"We don't go into that land. It's dangerous."

Jacob raised an eyebrow. "I know that now."

"You should have known it before, from your

bedtime lullabies."

"I didn't have that luxury," Jacob said.

"The Devil's March wasn't the road we told you to take."

"I improvised."

"Next time, don't."

"Next time, do it yourself." He stormed off and sat down aggressively on a rocky outcropping with his back towards everyone, with his back towards civilisation, and only the emptiness of the desert before him.

He heard Taberah follow him. "We're trying to do something good here."

"I'm not doing this for 'the cause,'" Jacob said.

"I think you are."

"Then you don't know me."

"I'm trying to get to know you, but you won't let me."

"Maybe it's safer that way."

"For who?"

"Both of us."

"I can take care of myself," Taberah stated.

"That's clear," Jacob replied bitterly. "Maybe only yourself."

Taberah glared at him, but he did not hold her gaze. He turned away from her, ignored her, and the power of that glare was diffused. He could hear her heavy breathing, could feel the hot air upon the side of his fair, as if she were unwittingly trying to burn his skin. Perhaps she tried to speak, to offer some rebuttal, some parrying rebuke, but all he heard was the sounds of her footsteps in the sand as they faded away from him.

Jacob sat there for another twenty minutes, sipping whiskey from his canister. No one bothered him except one of the men who unloaded the truck, a young lad not much older than Whistler, perhaps another of the Last.

"You know you really shouldn't anger her," he warned.

"Maybe she shouldn't anger me."

The man chuckled and shook his head. "You're made for each other."

Jacob shook his own head in turn. *She stands for different things*, he thought. *I don't stand for anything. I believe in nothing. I fight for no one.* He had told himself these things many times before, but now there was a difference: he felt a hint of doubt. Certainty was no longer his shield from the world.

When they returned to the Order's headquarters, Jacob meant to go immediately to Taberah's quarters, to offer some reluctant words of apology, to try to come to some sort of agreement about how they would part ways, how he would use his share of Ebronah's money to disappear to one of the western towns, where the Regime had less sway. But he was pulled aside by Teller, who was very eager to know how things had gone.

"You got them out, I take it?" Teller asked. He rubbed his hands together briskly.

"Them? You mean the coils?"

"Yes, the caskets, the crates. You got them out?"

"Yeah, I did my part."

"Did she offer you a share?"

"Ten percent."

"Beautiful," Teller said, and he gave his now familiar slimy grin. "You deserve it."

"I know," Jacob said. He felt a little on edge. "Did you need something?" he asked.

"No, no, I just wanted to congratulate you on a job well done, and commend you on your well-earned rewards." He slapped his greasy hand upon Jacob's back.

"Thank you," Jacob said. "If you'll excuse me."

When Jacob eventually made it to Taberah's quarters, he found she had just left and would not be back for hours. He sighed and sauntered back to his room, where he paced back and forth for a bit until he felt compelled to go to the cargo room, which was left unguarded, as if not a single person in the Order would dare steal a solitary coil.

"Ten percent," Jacob said to himself. "For what I did, for what I risked, it should have been more."

The light was dull in the room. Energy was a premium, and the Regime controlled most of the supply. Some was smuggled in like amulets. In the cargo room, however, there was only a single gaslight, just enough to see the shapes of the boxes. The crude silhouettes were somehow comforting. He almost did not want to disturb the shape.

He walked over to the nearest crate and pulled it towards him. He did not realise that the edge of another was resting upon it, and it crashed off the ground as it fell. He felt frustrated, as if somehow he was doing something wrong, as if he was really a thief rather than an exhausted worker coming to claim his rightful pay, a wage that would be denied him by his overbearing employer.

He cast aside those doubts just as he cast aside the fallen crate. He picked up the one he had earned. The weight was immense, and he struggled with it for a moment. He could hear the gentle chink of the coils inside, like the beginning of a melody.

He carried the crate, his crate, to the door, away from the gaslight, into the darkness that he much preferred. Something made him stop, and he turned as if he had heard another crate moving slightly. He saw nothing amiss. He looked at the crates, filled to the brim with cash. Cold cash, yet the kind of cash that warmed his soul.

He went back to the table and threw down the crate, where it clanged like his conscience. *The Resistance needs this*, he thought. *I don't need this money.*

He walked to the door, leaving the crate behind him. While he was no longer burdened by its weight, he felt an emptiness inside that only cash could fill. Now he understood more than ever where the money got its name, for it had coiled itself around his heart.

He turned sharply and gulped harshly. He barely realised he was clenching his fists, as if to stop them snatching any coils in sight. He wished he could roll a die to determine what to do, to put it in the hands of fate, but he had a feeling that he might re-roll if he did not like the result. The thought made him think of gambling, and made him desire the money even more, but another thought surfaced: that he was now gambling with his soul, and losing that was a heavier price.

He struggled for a time, and the battle with himself was harder than any he had fought against the Regime so far. He wished he could smuggle out the answer, smuggle a solution. In time the war was ended. Conscience is a powerful thing, but so is greed. Jacob seized the crate, his crate, his fortune, his reward.

I must have this, he told himself. *I have a right to it as much as anyone.* He clutched the crate tightly, like a mother holds a child. *I earned it*, which was true. *I need it*, which was a lie.

Chapter Twelve

PAYMENT

When Jacob met Taberah again, she still seemed angry, but this time she had a different focus for her anger.

"There's a crate missing," Taberah said. "Check the truck again."

"There's nothing missing," Jacob said. "You have your ninety percent."

"You mean you took a cut?"

"I deducted my payment, as agreed."

"I thought you weren't going to take it."

"You *hoped* I wouldn't," Jacob stated. "I told you I would."

"I'm disappointed in you," she said. Her words were like knives to his conscience, and as much as avarice dulled their blades, her tongue sharpened them. "That money was supposed to go to the war effort. Many people will die because of your decision, because of your selfishness."

Jacob tried to mask the shame; he hid it with defiance. "Yeah, well many people would have died if that money was spent on the tools of war."

"Many *demons* would die," Taberah corrected.

"Well, sometimes it's hard to tell the difference."

"Then stop looking in the mirror, Jacob," she said, and stormed off.

He stood alone, and he sighed deeply. In the silence it was harder to hide his guilt. In the solitude it was harder to bury his shame. He stood alone, and yet it felt as though someone was still berating him, like the echoes of those who had died at the hands of the Regime.

Taberah met with Rommond in her quarters, one of the few trips he made to the Order. It was almost always the other way around.

"Nine crates," Rommond said.

"Don't ask why there aren't ten."

"I wasn't going to. Nine is quite a haul."

"A thousand coils in each," Taberah said. "I was hoping for more."

"You're never satisfied, are you?"

"I won't be until the Regime is finished."

"I'm not sure you'll be satisfied even then," Rommond predicted.

They looked at each other as if they had had this conversation before, and there was disagreement in their eyes. Another conversation played out silently in their gaze, and it ended in a stalemate.

"So then," Taberah began.

"I won't field the Hopebreaker," Rommond interjected.

"When will you?" she asked, as if to imply it was a toy still in its packaging, as if Rommond was collecting soldiers while she was losing hers in war.

"When the time is right," Rommond replied. "I

cannot risk the Regime knowing what we have ... and getting access to more of our designs." He said this last part with great difficulty, as if the words were barbed.

"I know it hurts," Taberah said. "But you have to let him go."

Rommond ignored her. "Nine thousand coils. That will get you nine landships. They're old models, but they're fairly effective."

"Not as effective as the Hopebreaker."

"No, but we will need that for the future."

"If we have one, Rommond."

He placed both hands upon her shoulders and stared deeply into her eyes. "We are fighting for that future, Tabs."

"Why does it feel like I am fighting alone?" she asked. A solitary tear ran down her face.

Rommond did not seem moved. He had seen those tears before. He used guns in battle, but she used everything she had. "If you can only fight *your* way," he said, "you will always feel alone."

At that point, Jacob entered the room with Teller. Rommond gave Teller a dirty look, which Teller gave back with interest.

"Nice to see you again, Edward," Teller said with his taunting grin.

"And you, Reginald."

Jacob looked back and forth between the two men, and he could hear the gritting of teeth on each opposing side. "Bad blood?" he asked.

"You could say that," Rommond replied.

"He will say all sorts," Teller growled, pointing his

finger at the general as if it were a hexing wand. "He is the reason my face is on a poster in the first place!"

Rommond looked to Taberah, as if to suggest that if she did not throw Teller out, he would.

"Can you leave us, please, Teller?" Taberah asked.

Teller rolled his eyes. "Very well," he said, and he left as slowly as he could, eyeing Rommond as he went, as if his eyes were the barrels of guns.

"What was all that about?" Jacob asked when Teller had finally left.

"History," Rommond said.

"Teller isn't always easy to get on with," Taberah explained.

"You should have gotten rid of him years ago," Rommond said. "He's a liability."

"He's still useful, Rommond. We need everyone we can get."

"He seemed friendly enough to me," Jacob said. "A bit creepy, but I've met worse."

"Let's get back to business," Rommond said sternly.

Jacob scoffed. "All work and no play."

"War is not a game," Rommond said.

"Yet there are still winners and losers," Jacob said.

"Or just losers. No one truly wins a war."

"Ouch," Jacob said. "Is it national brooding day?"

"Whatever today is," Taberah said, "tomorrow is a day of reckoning."

"Attacking the Hope factory already?" Jacob asked.

"Will you be joining us, Jacob?" Taberah asked in turn. Her tone suggested the question was a mere formality. Jacob did not like the assumption that he was along for the ride.

"No," he stated. "I've done my bit. Smugglers aren't much use on the battlefield anyway."

Taberah was clearly taken aback. "You're giving up now?"

"I told you that this was it for me," he said.

"Go on," she scolded. "You're excused. Don't feel like you owe us anything."

"I don't," Jacob said.

"Go back to Blackout and sell the amulets we make. Profit from our work. Profit from those who have died to keep humanity alive. What good are those profits if we all fade away? What legacy will you leave behind but blemished gold?"

Jacob opened his mouth to speak, but shook his head instead. He walked off, and he almost felt like gesturing rudely as he went. Anger was in the striding of his legs, frustration in the movement of his arms. What was in his mind he could barely contain. He did not look to see what was in his heart.

He heard Rommond speak some words of consolement to Taberah, and some words of condemnation on Jacob's character, which only fuelled his frustration. He banged his fist on a metal panel lining one of the walls. The pain helped distract from the furore in his mind.

Screw them, he thought. *I don't owe them anything. I've done my bit. I've done more than most. This isn't my battle. This isn't my war.*

His mind was brought back to the crate of coils sitting in his quarters, his promise of a new life away from all the back-alley business, away from all the shadow deals, all the hiding and living in darkness, where he could never smuggle the light.

Profit was a powerful motivator—but so was a guilty conscience. He turned back and walked the walk of shame, back into the room where Taberah and Rommond stood. He took up a revolver. "Let's do this then."

Chapter Thirteen

LIGHTS OUT

R ommond had a treat for them outside the Order's
headquarters: nine of his war machines lined up
side-by-side. Unlike the more elegant design of the
Hopebreaker, these landships where rhomboidal
in shape, with metal tracks running all around the
chassis, and with sponsons protruding from either
side, in which a variety of gun turrets were positioned.
They were painted a dusty yellow-brown, to match
the desert, and most were badly chipped and scraped,
as if they had seen many battles before.

The sight of one landship was quite impressive,
but seeing nine of them in formation was almost
intimidating. Jacob had heard about machines
coming to life all by themselves in other parts of
Altadas, and he hoped that this would not be the case
with this platoon.

"All yours," Rommond said, but he rubbed the
hull of one of the landships as if he did not want to
give them up. "These are the Menacer Mark I's. They
aren't as well-balanced as newer models. It's why we
can't give them too much speed."

"Faulty vehicles," Jacob said. "Wonderful."

"Feel free to walk there instead," Rommond

suggested.

"It might be safer."

"With that mouth of yours, you might find nowhere's safe." Rommond turned to Taberah. "Keep them in good nick, Tabs. Don't go crazy with them. Consider them a loan, not a purchase. Bring as many back in one piece as you can manage."

"Will that be a Treasury loan?" Taberah jested.

Rommond was not amused. He rolled his shoulders as if to remove the hands of the Treasury's debt collectors. He eyed her severely as he walked away, and though he only glanced at Jacob, the glance was just as severe.

When Rommond was out of earshot, Taberah turned to Jacob. "Just so you know—"

"I know," Jacob interrupted with a huff. "There would be ten if it weren't for me."

Taberah raised an eyebrow. "I wasn't going to say that."

"But you were thinking it."

"Well, now I know *you* were," Taberah said.

Jacob feigned a grin in response.

"I was going to say," Taberah continued, "these beauties can take more of a beating." She tapped her knuckles on the hull of one, just as she had on the buckled hull of the battered steam truck.

"I'll bear that in mind," Jacob said.

Resistance drivers gave a very hurried training session to Order fighters, showing them the controls and weapon systems. Jacob was fine with the driving, but he could not quite get the hang of the sponson guns. Luckily there would be two people in each landship, and his assigned fighter, one of Taberah's elite called Andil, was much better at aiming and firing. They should have had two gunners, but the Order was short on soldiers, and was growing shorter after every mission.

As Jacob loaded his landship with supplies, he could not help but listen intently to Taberah's hushed conversation with Rommond at the next landship.

"So, one last time," Taberah said. "You won't be joining us?"

"No," Rommond said.

"I had to ask."

"I know."

Taberah looked away for a moment. "Maybe I should say this now, just in case."

"No," Rommond said. "No *just in case*. I want to see you back here, Tabs, with all my landships. That's an order, soldier."

Taberah smiled. "I don't follow orders."

"You never did," Rommond said. "But follow this one, please."

"I'll make it back," she said, but she did not seem certain. No one did.

They rolled out at sunset, one behind the other. Jameson, the most experienced landship driver, took the lead, followed by Taberah, followed by Jacob. Samadan, who was the most experienced with ambushes, took the rear.

Jacob could not really hear the sound of the other landships over the humming and cranking of his own.

He heard the whistle of steam coming from the pipes and the latching of the iron tracks as they clicked into place. He heard gears adjusting, the rhythm of the pumps, the revving of the engine, and the fuming of the furnace. He also heard Andil's heavy breathing, and he heard his own heart's heavy beating.

Sounds dominated everything, because there was little he could see. There was a small horizontal slit in the front of the vehicle, from which he could peer out, and there were other tiny openings throughout the hull, which let in small slivers of light. Otherwise there was darkness inside, so much so that he could not quite make out the features of Andil's face, only enough to know that he was apprehensive. He was glad the landship did not have any mirrors.

Darkness fell upon the dunes, sapping the yellows and reds, replacing the grains with the overwhelming blanket of black. While Jacob was comfortable in the darkness, he felt more than a little claustrophobic in his metal cage, and he found driving more difficult, because now he was following the tiny flicker of fire that emerged from the cracks of the vehicle ahead. He did not know if they had lit an oil lamp, or if it was just the light of the furnace, but he was glad that it was there, and he tried not to block the light of his own furnace, to avoid a pileup of landships behind him.

For much of the journey in the darkness the pale flicker was not enough to guide him, and the smoke and steam that each landship released was no help, so he had to strain his hearing to catch the revving of other engines and the turning of their tracks.

"We hadn't quite planned for this darkness," Jacob whispered to Andil.

"We did," Andil whispered back. "Believe me. It's better this way."

Suddenly the tiny glimmer of fire from the landship ahead went out, and the sounds died off suddenly, as if the darkness had consumed all things.

"Stop and douse!" Andil whispered harshly, and he took a bucket of water to the furnace, which hissed angrily as its fires flickered out. Jacob pulled the vehicle to a halt, and he glanced through one of the peepholes in the back to see that the other fires were being swiftly snuffed out.

"What's wrong?" Jacob asked.

Andil shushed him. In the tiny glimmer of light that the embers cast, Jacob could see that Andil was hugging his legs, and that his hands were trembling. Jacob bit his lip to stop it following suit. He was not certain if he should peer outside or just stare at the disturbing shadows on the inside of the chassis. He hoped with fervour that nothing was staring back.

It seemed like an agonising wait, made all the more agonising by the enforced silence. His mind screamed at him, and his tongue tried to defy his belligerent lips. He thought that perhaps that was another reason why he bit them so fiercely.

Suddenly there was a deafening screech, louder than any Jacob had ever heard before. He covered his ears, and he saw that Andil had done the same, but Andil's hands shook even more violently than before, as if he was fighting off an attacker that assaulted with sound. Another cry of metal sounded outside, followed by a phenomenal thump, which shook the ground and shook the landships, and shook anyone inside who was not already shaking.

Several more thuds struck the ground, each one growing fainter and farther away, until eventually the sounds were very distant, yet no less terrifying. Even when silence returned from wherever it sought refuge, the sounds continued to echo in all minds.

"What was that?" Jacob whispered, much lower than before.

"A Behemoth," Andil said.

"It sounded big."

"It is."

Jacob glanced outside to see if he could see any of this Behemoth, but the darkness refused to reveal the monster, and perhaps his eyes refused to see it. A new flicker of fire appeared in the landship in front, and he heard the engines roar into action, followed by the rhythm of the pumps and the revolving tracks. He started up his own vehicle, but this time he was a lot less confident than before.

They continued their journey for a time, winding along the dusty roads that were usually travelled by the Regime instead. It was a daring mission, and a daunting journey, and it seemed that the night only thickened, and the darkness only strengthened. Then Jacob saw the flashing of a lamp from the landship ahead, which was his signal to break formation and enter a new one, where all of the vehicles lined up side by side. Jacob knew what this meant: that they were near the Hope factory.

"Now it's your time to work," Jacob said to Andil.

"Oh, you'll be working too, don't worry."

"I'm not worried," Jacob said, but he was not sure he believed himself.

They drove in this new formation for half an hour, with no light ahead to lead them, and no light behind to reassure them that something else was not on their trail. Instead the pale lights of their comrades were on either side, where the drivers could not see them, but where the gunners took some small encouragement. In the battle ahead, they would need it.

For a moment Jacob thought he heard something else driving beside him that he had not heard before. It sounded old and clunkier, like a landship that had seen better days. He dismissed the sound, presuming it was one of his comrades, but he began to wonder if some of Rommond's treasured vehicles were breaking down before they reached their destination. He began instinctively looking for faults in his own Menacer Mark I, but everything seemed in good order. Everything bar his gut feeling, everything bar his suspicions.

"Stop for a moment," Andil called. He was peering intently out of a slit in the sponson, with his fingers gripping tightly the trigger of the gun.

"What is it?"

"I don't know," Andil answered.

"Not a Behemoth, I hope."

Andil did not respond, which was not reassuring. The lack of tremors in the ground helped a lot, but the silence and uncertainty did not.

"I'm seeing small flashes of light on our right

flank," Andil explained.

Jacob took a look and then glanced out the peephole on the left sponson, and he saw them there too. "Maybe they're warnings."

"But warnings of what?" Andil asked.

Before Jacob could answer, he heard again the humming of a vehicle pass by. He looked out quickly and caught a glimpse of it before it passed. It looked like another Menacer Mark I, but it was hard to make much out in the darkness. One thing that was odd, however, was that it seemed to be going in the wrong direction.

"I see a Mark I going back," Jacob said in bewilderment.

Andil looked up with anxious eyes. "Maybe the lights are a signal to retreat."

Jacob shook his head. "I can't see Taberah ordering a retreat. This raid is too important."

"You have no idea what kind of equipment the Regime has."

"I'd like to find out and destroy some of it."

"Turn back," Andil said. "If the others are retreating, we need to turn back."

"No," Jacob said, and he was glad that he was driving. He hoped Andil was not this hesitant when it came to firing. "This doesn't make any sense. We're so close. We can't turn back now."

He fired up the landship once more and rolled slowly forward, despite frequent pleas from Andil, who reported that the flashing lights had stopped. He took this as a sign that all their allies were gone, that they were out there in the darkness alone.

Suddenly there was a booming sound to the far right, followed by an explosion, which illuminated the area briefly, revealing the silhouettes of far more than nine landships on the field of battle. There were dozens of them, and many of them had different, more intimidating silhouettes than the Menacer Mark I.

"There are ... we're outnumbered," Andil stuttered.

"Then thin them out, Andil! Fire!"

Andil's mouth may have been hesitant, but his fingers were not. The stutter of his words was quickly followed by the stutter of the gun, and suddenly the entire field erupted in gunfire and explosions, and the loud and angry revving of engines as landships turned sharply in the darkness and the dust.

Jacob responded to Andil's feverish cries, which told him where to turn and by how many degrees. When Andil ordered a full stop, Jacob took up sentry in the left sponson, firing a volley here and there at the Regime landships, many of which were larger and more box-shaped than those of the Resistance. He did not like firing the gun, because it meant he was not moving the vehicle, and he felt like every passing second was sharpening the focus of the enemy's crosshairs.

Another Mark I passed in front of him, clunking loudly as it went, and Jacob managed to stop his trigger finger just in time. In that split second, he thought that Taberah might be in that one, and maybe she stopped firing at him in the nick of time as well.

But something else triggered in his mind. He

thought he caught a fleeting glimpse of a symbol on the side of the passing landship: a black square upon a red cross, the emblem of the Regime.

"Damn it!" Jacob cried. "They've got the same landships as us!"

"How are we going to know who to shoot at?" Andil asked.

"We'll have to be extra careful," Jacob replied, and he knew that Andil shared his fear: that they might have already killed some of their comrades. "We'll need to look for their insignia."

"I can barely see the landships, never mind the insignia!"

"Then we'll have to get closer," Jacob said. "And let's hope they can't see us that well either."

Jacob jumped back into the driving seat and set the landship in motion, using the steering sticks to turn sharply at random intervals, in case they were ever in the enemy's line of sight. He was not sure if Taberah or the others had noticed the Regime's Menacer I contingent, but he knew the battle was still ongoing, with explosions rocking the landscape, and smoke filling his vision through the view port.

Andil fired steadily at targets that entered his view. Jacob brought them very close to other landships, dangerously close, but close enough that Andil could see if they were friend or foe. On most occasions the encounter ended with a barrage of bullets, but here and there Jacob was glad that Andil's finger did not twitch upon the trigger.

They continued this deadly dance across the battlefield, played to the music of gunfire, which rattled them as much as it rattled the hulls of almost every landship in sight, and almost every one they could not turn quickly enough to see. Then the music took a bullet of its own, for Jacob no longer heard the song of Andil's gun. He glanced at Andil and realised he was not moving. The man was slumped over the gun, dripping blood as quickly as the gun bled bullets.

But Jacob had no time to think, nor time to grieve. Ahead of him was another of the Regime's rectangular landships, chugging slowly into place. Its turret was facing the other way, but it was slowly creaking towards him.

Jacob turned sharply and leapt out of his seat. He pushed Andil from the turret, shoved the gunner from his grave. The body slumped to the floor, and Jacob seized the blood-covered trigger. This would not be a metal mausoleum for the both of them.

But the turret jammed, and no amount of force seemed to move it. Jacob knew that if he fired now, it would miss the mark. He pulled it back to the right and slammed it to the left, and he heard a click and a clang, and he fired before even looking at his target. An explosion echoed outside, and he glanced out at the black smoke to see that he had destroyed the Regime landship. He also saw, with a mix of horror and relief, that its own turret was just one final movement from finding its mark.

Yet there was no time to rejoice for the living or mourn for the dead. He jumped back in the driving seat, only to be greeted by an even more horrifying sight. He saw another monstrous landship before him, bigger than the Menacer Mark I, with a large turret on the top. He did not have much time to look, however, for he saw that the turret was aimed straight at him. In that split second he knew he could not drive out of the way in time, or turn the landship to aim and fire either of the guns. He only had enough time to begin to get out of his seat when he felt as though the entire landship had been thrown back several metres, and him along with it. He banged off one of the panels inside and scalded his hand upon the furnace, and he had barely managed to stand up again when he realised that there was more smoke inside than before. He turned back and saw that flames had engulfed the mangled hull, and he knew that there was only seconds to get out before they would engulf him too.

It only took a single glance to realise that the entry hatch upon the roof was badly buckled, and that he would never be able to unlock it. He reached immediately for the escape hatch in the floor of the vehicle, but it was jammed shut. He began to kick it furiously to try to open it, but it only budged a little. He began to feel the heat intensify, and he knew that the flames were inching closer to him, a new enemy that would consume him. He grabbed the shovel from the furnace and tried to wedge it between the tiny gap between the escape hatch and the main hull, but it would not fit. He looked around for the toolbox and found it tucked behind Andil's body, knocked there from the force of the enemy's turret fire. Jacob opened the box and began to root through, and even as he did, and even as the fires crept closer, and the smoke became thicker, he hoped to all gods, even those he did not believe in, that the enemy landship would not fire again.

He found a crowbar buried deep inside the toolbox, and used it to force the escape hatch open. The small square opening was barely enough to fit the thinnest of people through, but there was something about the threat of imminent death that made the tightest of spots swift to squeeze through. As his torso popped through the hatch, leaving only his head to feel the heat and flames, he thought for a moment of reaching back in and pulling Andil out, but the thought was soon smothered by the smoke, extinguished by the fire, and all he could do was duck under the hull of the landship and crawl in the muck beside the tracks.

When Jacob emerged at the back of his Menacer Mark I, he tried to keep close to its burning hull to avoid being run over or shot by enemy landships, but the heat forced him out more into the open, as did the thought of the entire thing exploding and sending shrapnel and flames in pursuit of him. He had barely stepped a few feet away from his refuge when he heard the engine of another landship as it rolled up beside him. It was another Menacer Mark I, and from his blurred vision he could not quite make out its insignia. The guns turned to point at him, the sound of their adjustment like the prelude of a death knell. Jacob raised his hands, though he was not entirely sure surrender would save him. He heard a loud click and thought that this was it, the trigger of his death. Then the hatch opened and a figure stood up.

"I'll take the cost of that landship from your earnings," the figure said, and though Jacob's vision was still blurred and the smoke billowed to every part of the battlefield, he knew that the voice was that of Taberah.

Chapter Fourteen

FORTRESS HOPE

"I'll have to stop rescuing you," Taberah said.

"I think I rescued myself," Jacob replied defiantly. He still held the crowbar tightly, as if his hands instinctively knew that he might have to escape again.

Taberah smiled. "Get in."

"Andil didn't—"

"He knew what he signed up for," Taberah said.

"I'm not sure I did," Jacob said. "What will we do about him?"

"Never mind him," Taberah said. "Get in."

Jacob complied, and he felt the heat propel him forward, as if the flicking flames had come from her tongue.

It was cramped inside the landship, even more than usual, and yet these vehicles were designed for three people: one driver and two gunners. Jacob preferred to drive, but he knew for certain that Taberah would not hand over that duty. He brushed off Soasa, who clutched her sponson gun as if it fired a thousand tiny bombs. He winked at her as he passed.

"Cosy," Jacob said as he bumped up against Taberah while making his way to the second gun position in the right sponson.

"Don't get too comfortable," Taberah said. "Dawn is breaking."

There was something about that last word that Jacob did not like. Perhaps it was because it was often followed by *bones*. And there was something about dawn he did not like either. Perhaps it was because it chased away the shadows he felt more comfortable hiding in.

The battle of the darkness was over, and only four of Rommond's landships were left standing, but who knew what battles the light would bring, and how many would survive them. The sun pushed through the cracks of night, and as the shadows crumbled, new shadows rose up to reflect the pinnacles of the Hope factory, to highlight the monstrosities that invaded the clouds.

Taberah led them into the factory complex, bulldozing barbed wire as if it was cotton string. Were it not for the Hope factories seeing so much traffic, with transports pouring in and out by the dozen, the ground might have been laced with land mines. This was the only occasion where they were thankful that Hope was in demand.

The landship had taken a beating, leaving the gear sticks in bad shape. Taberah struggled with them, and the vehicle jerked forward, and when it was not lurching it was so sluggish that Jacob thought he could walk faster. Hell, he could crawl quicker.

He held back his instinct to seize the steering sticks and show her how it was done, and he bit back many tips and suggestions, until finally he could no longer take the ponderous pace. The landship might have had a shell, but that did not mean it had to move like a snail.

"Pull the gear stick back and to the right before pushing it forward again," Jacob suggested.

"I tried that," Taberah said. "It didn't work."

"Try it to the—"

"*I'm* driving this vehicle," Taberah snapped, "not you."

He gave a sheepish glance at her, and he noticed her reluctantly and secretly trying his technique. It took a few attempts, but eventually the gear stick slid into place, and the tank doubled in speed. Given how slow they were previously going, that was not a huge increase.

"You might be fast, Jacob," Taberah said. "But I get my vehicles to their destination in one piece."

Soasa laughed as if she had suppressed many laughs at his expense before. Jacob could almost hear her etching score marks in her brain. Taberah-1, Jacob-0.

They parked in the largely empty grounds of the factory complex. There were few transports there, and fewer guards. Those few fell quickly to Soasa's well-aimed grenades. The surviving Order soldiers left the safety of their metal cabins and entered the metal mansion that fed the Regime.

The production halls were more amazing on the inside than the entire factory was on the outside. Huge and elaborate machinery were in place, with many production belts, robotic arms, pistons and pumps, and an endless supply of steam, which masked the uppermost parts of the factory machinery like clouds mask the heavens. It was here that the industry of Hope flourished.

The drug itself was plentiful to see, lying in large vats, where it was stirred above great fires, and also in numerous bags and crates, each labelled and ready for shipping to one of the Regime's numerous controlled or occupied cities, where the demons craved this sustenance, where they would wither and die without it.

There were few people in this particular chamber, and they were largely oblivious to the intruders. It only took a single glance to realise that they were not Regime workers, earning a fair wage and a decent living, but slaves from across the Regime's occupied territory. They were all shapes and sizes, and yet all of them hunched over, tending to their singular duty, and gradually sinking lower and closer to the ground that would be their final fate. They paid no heed to the trespassers, because they had been made part of the factory itself, another piston in the machine, another cog in the wheel, and they focused only on their ordained task, their obsession, their drug.

"This is so sad," Jacob said. "We have to free them."

"We're not here for a rescue mission," Taberah replied. "We need to blow up the factory."

"But can't we get them out as well?"

Soasa scoffed. "He's clueless."

"They've been broken, Jacob," Taberah explained. "There's nothing of them left to save."

Jacob felt more than a little helpless when Taberah and Soasa began to lead teams throughout the complex with wires and explosives. Here and there he tripped over those same wires and was always thankful he did not trip over the explosives as well. He stood and watched, and he could not help but turn his attention to the slaves, who continued to make the provender of their captors. In another world, this might have been him. Hell, in this world, it could still be him.

He saw one of Taberah's younger soldiers, Orga, struggling to untie a length of wire. She looked around nervously, and she became even more nervous when Jacob tried to help her.

"Relax," he said, but it was as much a command to his own body as hers.

He barely had time to run the length of wire before he was dragged away by Taberah, and the group huddled in the corner behind a mass of pistons, which looked as though they had come together to share their tales, to share their steam. It seemed that in this place the machinery did the talking, while those of flesh and blood toiled, each one just another mechanism in the great factory of life and death.

"So then," Soasa said. "Let this be a message to the Regime."

"More than a message," Taberah corrected. "More than a warning. Let it be the start of the avalanche that buries this demon scum forever."

If they were not so deep inside an enemy complex they might have cheered. Even so, there was a noticeable rejoicing in the eyes of all present, mixed with a hint of apprehension as Taberah's finger hovered over the button.

Jacob felt his eyes begin to squint in expectation, and his shoulders began to rise, as if to shield his head. He never liked explosions and loud noises. He preferred the quiet, the silent stalking that made smuggling possible. Yet he knew well that such noises often proved a welcome distraction—only this time it would draw attention to where he and the Order's raiding party stood.

And then the sound came, but it was more subdued than he expected. In that blink he did not see what had transpired, but he heard a bang, followed by a cry from Taberah, and then a great commotion as people scrambled here and there to duck for cover. Jacob joined them on the floor, where he found Taberah, cradling her bloody hand, in which was impaled a bullet. Several more bullets pelted past, striking the metal grating of the floor, and some of them ricocheted back and forth, and some of them struck the fleeing bodies of the Order's soldiers.

Jacob managed to crawl closer to Taberah and drag her out of the line of fire, and just in time, for a round of bullets hit the place where she previously lay. He pulled her up and placed her back against a large piston, and he realised that another bullet was embedded in her shoulder.

"Damn it," Jacob said. "They got you good."

"No," she whispered, and she rubbed her hand across her chest and stomach, as if searching for other bullets. "They missed."

Jacob shook his head. Perhaps he was denying

that this was happening, that they had gotten so close and yet still failed. Perhaps he was denying the blood permission to leave Taberah's body. Perhaps he was denying her permission to die.

Then he heard the sound of heavy boots upon the metal grating behind him. He froze, and he heard the click of a gun. He expected Taberah to look up to the figure, but she looked away instead.

"Don't move," the man behind him said.

"I'm not," Jacob replied.

He felt the whack of the gun on the back of his neck, but he tried not to show his pain.

"Turn around," the guard ordered. There was something about the accent of the Regime's men that made everything sound like an order. *Live. Die. Flee. Never fight. Never resist.* The Regime ordered people to do it all.

"Which is it?" Jacob asked. "Move or don't move?"

Another whack, and another surge of pain, built upon the bones of the last one. Jacob held his breath for a moment and then let it out very slowly, as if he had been ordered to breathe. He turned around even slower. If he was going to give in, he would only give a little.

When his eyes adjusted to the light of the torch that was pointed at his face, he faltered a little, for there before him, towering above him in his thick leather coat and black uniform, with the emblem of the Regime on his left shoulder, stood a most familiar figure. *Domas.* Jacob was surprised he did not say the name aloud.

"You didn't think it would be that easy, did you?"

Domas asked. He pointed the torch straight into Jacob's face, making it harder for his eyes. Domas knew he preferred the shadow.

"It wasn't," Jacob said.

"Don't answer him," Taberah insisted.

Domas ignored her as much as she ignored him. He strode closer to Jacob and grabbed him by the throat. "Let me assure you, smuggler, that things are about to get much more difficult."

Chapter Fifteen

FORTRESS DESPAIR

It was not long before all of the Order's people were rounded up and herded together, like stray animals that had wandered into the factory that would ultimately process them. Jacob shuddered at the thought, but he could not shake it entirely from his mind.

Even as they huddled together, not knowing what might follow, and fearing that unknown eventuality, more Regime soldiers surrounded them, and it seemed to Jacob that they had been there all the time, waiting to reveal themselves.

"We thought you might try something like this," Domas told them smugly, priding himself on this expert deduction, as if he was the mastermind behind it all. "You're not the first to storm a Hope factory."

"And we won't be the last," Jacob said.

Domas smiled with his eyes. "I hope not. I'll be waiting for all of them."

He paced back and forth across the grating, his boots mimicking the rhythms of the pumps and the pistons, and even when he stopped he seemed agitated, and he twitched and turned, and he looked this way and that, and it seemed that he had to keep moving, as if stillness were death. Jacob found it very irritating, as if Domas' own agitation were contagious.

"What will you do with us?" Orga asked. Taberah glowered at her, and she did not ask any more questions, and she kept her gaze to the ground, in case her eyes might ask some more.

"I haven't decided yet," Domas said with great pleasure, as if the various options were all delightful to him in their own way. Jacob was certain that he would find them anything but delightful.

"If you had succeeded," Domas explained, "then many of us would have starved. The city of Blackout would have been host to a famine created by the Resistance, and I think your support would have weakened as much as the bodies of our poor children. Yet the Iron Empire would go on, for there are six more Hope factories in Altadas, so perhaps your plan was altogether too … hopeful."

Jacob rolled his eyes. Part of him tried to hide it, but another part wanted Domas to see. There really was nothing like defiance. What Hope was to the demons, defiance was to the prisoner. It was its own kind of sustenance.

"They were like you once," Domas said, pointing to the slaves who continued to work, and who continued to waste away as they toiled. "They came with their own kind of hope, and some hoped to escape, and some hoped to defy the Iron Empire, and some even hoped to topple the Iron Emperor, but those that did not leave were broken, and those that left … were dead."

"I think he plans to bore us to death," Jacob said.

He looked to the others for a chuckle, but he did not find it. Domas was the only one who entertained him.

Domas walked to one of the giant vats, dipped his finger in the powder and held it before Jacob's eyes, as if he wanted him to taste it. "Hard to believe, isn't it, that something so innocuous could be so powerful?" He licked it slowly from his finger, ingesting every last granule, and the look in his eyes showed that it was not just powerful—it was pleasurable.

Domas rested his large gloved hand upon a lever close to Jacob. Too close.

"Pull the lever," the general commanded.

"No," Jacob responded.

Domas replied with a fist. "I want you to help create what you tried to destroy," he said. "I want you to know that it was by your hands that we thrive."

"You want a lot of impossible things," Jacob said, "and you call me hopeful."

The gloves did not cushion the blows. Maybe they enhanced them.

"Just do it, for heaven's sake," Orga said. The pain in Jacob's face begged the same. But the heavens never helped Jacob before. Hell, it was from the heavens that the demons came.

"Listen to her, smuggler," Domas said. "She has more wisdom than you."

Jacob continued to defy him, and so Domas turned his attention to Taberah. He crouched down beside her, almost on top of her, until his breath steamed up the metal piston she leaned against. He drew disturbingly close, as if he were about to reveal something very intimate, but Taberah did not look at him. Jacob wanted to grab him off her, and the Regime soldiers must have noticed his irritation, for several of them pointed their guns at him. He could not defy bullets.

"It's been a while, hasn't it?" Domas whispered to Taberah, blowing the words upon her face. She kept a level gaze, ignoring him. "They say time helps you forget, but I haven't forgotten you, Taberah. I don't think you've forgotten me either." Still she ignored him, though Jacob could see that it was not easy, that her defiance was more difficult than his own.

Domas ran his gloved fingers up Taberah's left arm like a spider. It was a gentle, but unsettling, touch. Taberah bit her lip to hold back a grimace. Domas' molesting fingers reached her shoulder, where the bullet from his own gun was lodged, and he ran his index finger around the wound, as if invoking the genie of death that was previously trapped in the barrel of his gun.

"Did I hurt you?" he asked, and he feigned compassion, and to all ears it was obvious that it was feigned. Taberah continued her meditative glare, and yet Jacob thought that at any moment she might snap, and Domas' neck might follow suit.

"How's Rommond?" Domas asked. "You don't like me asking about him, do you? We know he's still alive. We know you know where. It's only a matter of time, Taberah, only a matter of time."

Domas gently lifted up Taberah's left hand, until she cringed from the pain in her shoulder, and he placed her hand delicately upon the lever. He patted it softly, and he smiled a sickly smile. "Pull the lever," he whispered to her like a lover.

She defied him with her silence and stillness, and Jacob applauded her in his mind, and yet part of him was growing increasingly concerned. He realised he almost was not breathing.

Taberah did not pull the lever. Her hand rested on it like the hand of a doll.

Suddenly Domas slammed his hand against the piston she leaned against, and she blinked, but she did not budge, and her hand remained limp. "Pull the lever," Domas urged like an ex-lover hoping to get back into her bed.

Still she resisted, and the more she defied him, the less gentle he was.

"I'll do it," Jacob volunteered.

Domas took Taberah's hand and placed it on her thigh, where he kept his own hand for a time. He hovered close to her for a moment more, just breathing on her skin, before he finally withdrew and stood up. He turned to Jacob and raised his chin, and smiled.

"It is easier to comply than to resist," he said. "So there is wisdom in you after all."

Jacob struggled to hold back a response. If Taberah was not there, he might not have struggled, no matter the price to him.

"Do it," Domas ordered. "Feed the hungry."

Jacob reluctantly placed his hand on the lever and pushed it down. The machinery creaked into action around them, and a new batch of Hope was made.

Domas took a taste of this batch. "It tastes even better knowing that you made it," he said.

There was a sudden thud a few metres away near one of the Hope vats. All eyes were drawn to it, where they saw one of the slaves slumped dead upon the ground.

"Looks like we have a dropper," Domas said. "They say you shouldn't see how the food is made, but you like defiance, so maybe we should defy that advice."

They were herded towards the slaughter chambers, and they knew where they were heading, despite no announcements and no signs, for the sounds that came from that place, the drills and saws, etched their way into the chambers of their minds.

Yet the sounds did not prepare them for what awaited them. When they entered through the large double doors, the handles of which were spattered with blood, they saw great racks of bodies hanging up, and the slave who had just died was being added to a new hook.

"This isn't the secret ingredient," Domas said. "It's just the spice."

Orga tried to run from the room, but they stopped her, and they held her back, but she could not hold back her tears and tremors. Jacob held her up, and she buried her head in his chest, and perhaps she tried to bury the images she had seen.

"Enough play," Domas said.

He must have said those words a thousand times before, because the guards knew what they meant. They seized each of them and dragged them back into the production hall, where they were tied up one by one, whether they kicked and fought, as Jacob did, or wept and wailed, as Orga did, or screamed and shouted, as many others did. Taberah did not fight, and did not scream, and did not weep. It seemed that she had resigned herself to her fate, had come to terms with death. Jacob could not help but get the impression that she had done so a long time before.

Orga was taken up first and hung above one of the vats of Hope. Before it cooled and dried into a fine white powder, it formed a thick black liquid. In this state, where it bubbled and blistered ferociously, Jacob could not help but dub it Despair.

"Let her go!" Jacob shouted, but they did not listen to him.

They began to slowly submerge her, and she kicked and screamed, until they no longer saw her kicking and no longer heard her screams.

Then the others were hung up, one by one, and Jacob was strung up beside them, and he tried to resist, but they overpowered him with ease. There were no shadows to slip into, and even if there were, he was not sure he could leave Taberah behind.

She was the only one they did not string up. "We'll save you for later," Domas said.

As Jacob hung there, trying to copy Taberah's ability to block out everything around her, trying to close his ears to the sounds of the screams on either side of him, and trying to blot out his peripheral vision to those dipping hooks and submerging bodies, he stared out of the window that faced him, and he saw the red desert under the morning sun, that same desert that had been created by the Regime's invasion of this world. Those sands did not look evil, and though the sun could be oppressive, its heat was not always unwelcome. It was now as much a home to the Resistance as it was the Regime. As Jacob stared at this, he wondered what new desert he would travel to in death, what new desert he would make his home.

Then Jacob saw a dark blot upon the horizon. It could have been anything, but something about it gave him hope. Even as his arms were bound, and he hung above the boiling liquid, and any other person would give in to despair, he watched the shape growing larger in the distance. In time it was close enough that he could make out the details, and by this time others were staring at it and making eager cries. The Regime soldiers turned to it too, but they were not so eager.

There, flanked on either side by many different landships, was the Hopebreaker.

Chapter Sixteen

THE IRON CAVALRY

Jacob barely had time to smile before the building rocked and the windows exploded, and there was the rattle of gunfire and the steady booming of great turret guns, and beneath these ear-rending noises was the sound of panicked voices and hurried feet as the Regime soldiers raced out to meet their attackers.

Domas left with the others, but as he ran for the exit he fired several shots at those hanging above the vats, and many of them hit their mark, but Jacob managed to shimmy out of the way of the bullet that came his way.

Taberah freed herself from her bonds, and then she hurriedly pushed buttons and pulled levers to try to free her companions, and sometimes they helped, but other times they fired up more machinery, which brought each of them closer to their doom.

"I don't mean to rush you," Jacob said, "but I'm starting to really feel this heat."

Some more button presses and lever pulling dropped him several inches closer to the vat.

"Eh, that's warmer."

"If you shut up and let me do what I'm doing, maybe I'll do it quicker."

Jacob could see from his vantage point that the controls were very unusual. The slaves might have had the rest of their lives to learn them, but Taberah only had a few minutes, if even that. It was trial and error, and Jacob did not like that his life, or his death, would be decided by guesswork.

"Over here!" Soasa called, and she kicked towards a lever marked with an arrow pointing to the left. "I think this moves us down on the conveyor belt."

Taberah clambered over to the lever and pulled it down, and Soasa's guess proved right, for all of them hanging above the vats jolted and were moved one place to the left, and then the machine stopped, and they were left dangling above the ground instead.

"Okay, that's better," Jacob said. "Now, hit that one that dropped us down before."

"I can't remember which one that was," Taberah cried, and she raced back to the main control panel.

"The black one with the yellow stripes," Jacob said. "I think."

His own guess was right as well, and they were lowered down to the ground, where Taberah could remove them from the hooks and untie their hands.

"My saviour," Jacob said. He was not entirely sarcastic.

"Thank me later," Taberah replied.

Jacob smiled. "Oh, I will."

He helped get the others down, and when they were all free he grabbed one of the slaves by the shoulders. He looked very young, and very thin and frail, and he reminded Jacob a lot of Whistler, which made it more difficult when the man stared back with blank eyes and tried to go back to work.

"Come on!" he cried. "You're free."

But he did not come, and not one among the others stirred even a little from their duties. Jacob realised that there could be no prison walls and no prison guards, and they would still never be free. He would rather die than live like that, but few people caught by the Regime had the luxury of that choice. For many, they would live as slaves, and then would die, and those who toiled side by side with them would end up mixing them into the very substance they worked to create.

All of this hit Jacob deep inside more than anything else the Regime had done, more than any of the tales of their cruelty and oppression. Rumours of genocide compared little with the sight of it. To see people butchered and broken could butcher the heart and break the spirit.

The workers were dazed in their servitude, but Jacob was dazed by their seeming unwillingness to fight or run, or do anything but what their masters ordered them to do. He stood there for a moment, feeling he should do something, but not knowing what to do. Then Taberah grabbed him by the arm and pulled him with her to where the other Order members raided a supply cabinet for guns.

"There's not much ammunition here," Soasa said.

"We'll have to make every bullet count," Taberah replied.

She shoved a rifle into Jacob's hands. It helped remove a little of his feeling of helplessness, and he tried not to look back at the slaves, in case he would be ensnared by their plight again. Taberah must have noticed his struggle. "Forget them," she told him. "We have our own battle to fight."

They left the production hall, ducking low as parts of the factory came apart under the constant fire of Rommond's iron army.

Rommond drove the Hopebreaker straight towards the Hope factory, ordering his men to fire as he went. The loaders and gunners operated swiftly and expertly, and a new shell was ready even as the old one struck the factory walls. As they fired, the landship cruised across the desert floor as if it were a steady sea.

"10 o'clock," Rommond called out calmly as an enemy Menacer Mark I came into view. The sight of the Regime's emblem on the Resistance-designed vehicle caused a little twitch in Rommond's right eye, but that was the extent that he would show his discomfiture.

The turret swivelled around, and the gunner locked his target. The enemy landship was destroyed in seconds, sending plumes of smoke into the air to join the numerous plumes of the Hope factory.

"Straight ahead," Rommond said as another came into view. This one fired a shot before it was destroyed, but the shell simply bounced off the hull of the Hopebreaker, and neither Rommond nor his men flinched at the sound.

"Right flank!" one of the gunners cried, and Rommond turned the landship sharply, adjusting his periscope until he could see a Behemoth before him.

It was a massive rectangular vehicle supported both by giant legs and tracks, and it easily towered over the Hopebreaker. Anyone else who faced it might have fled, but Rommond accelerated towards it, and the gunners fired as he went.

The Behemoth creaked loudly, and there was an unholy sound of spinning cogs and pummelling pumps, as if it were a factory of its own. Hatches opened and large guns emerged, and they all aimed at the Hopebreaker as it whizzed around the monstrous vehicle.

"Incoming," Rommond said, and before he even finished the word, there was a steady pelting against the hull. But inside, it sounded like nothing more than rain, and Rommond treated it like the mere annoyance of the weather, even though it very rarely rained in Altadas any more.

The Behemoth had more than bullets in its arsenal, however, and as the Hopebreaker circled it once, Rommond noticed that there were larger hatches opening, which produced larger guns. Even as he passed one of these by, he saw that it was attached to massive tanks of oil.

"Flamethrowers on both sides," he said. "Full about."

He stopped the Hopebreaker even as the first flamethrower began to spit out massive jets of flame. He turned sharply and began to drive in the opposite direction, but even as he did so, and even as his gunners continued to fire upon the Behemoth, destroying many of the gun positions around it, Rommond noticed that the hull of the Behemoth was raising up upon a circular platform.

"Behemoth rotation," he told his men, and they braced themselves for another sharp stop as Rommond turned the Hopebreaker around once more and began circling it the other way. Even as he did so, the Behemoth's hull began to rotate around on its tracks, and the flamethrowers followed the landship, turning the red sands to black. Were it not for the Hopebreaker's unrivalled speed, it would have smouldered black as well.

The machine gunners proved ineffective against the flamethrowers, but the main turret was turned around to fire at them as Rommond continued to speed away from the pursuing flames. Though those flames barely lapped at the hull of the landship, he began to feel the heat increase inside.

A Menacer Mark III from Rommond's army joined him in the fight against the Behemoth, but it had barely come into range and fired a series of shots before it was caught in the path of the flamethrower and destroyed in seconds.

Another shell ricocheted off the flamethrower turret, exploding in the air.

"Another miss!" the gunner cried.

"Target the oil tanks," Rommond called.

"I can't get a proper shot!"

"Take over for me," Rommond said. The gunner took the driving seat, while Rommond settled into the seat of the turret gunner. The leather was warm, but the air inside the landship was getting warmer.

"Ready to fire, General," the loader confirmed.

Rommond took his time to carefully line up a

shot, readjusting several times as the Hopebreaker jolted when it struck a rock jutting out of the sandy wastes. He could only see a small part of the oil tanks, and he knew that there was no direct line of fire, so he aimed instead for the back of the hatch that contained those tanks, and hoped that the shell would bounce off it to cause an explosion inside.

He fired, and there was a huge explosion inside the Behemoth. The flamethrower coughed up its last flames, but new flumes of fire spat out from the main hull as the explosion caused a chain reaction inside. The spinning hull ground to a halt, and Regime soldiers jumped out, some of them engulfed in flames.

"You almost pity them," Lieutenant Tradam said.

"I don't," Rommond answered. "This is what happens when you play with fire."

Rommond took back control of the steering sticks and drove alongside the fleeing Regime soldiers, and they were gunned down as they ran, but here and there one of those on fire was allowed to run as far as the fire would let them—and it was not far.

"Let them burn," Rommond said. The twitch in his eye had long stopped by now.

When the Behemoth was destroyed, and its occupants were dead or dying, Rommond began to head back towards the factory complex, which crumbled from the shelling.

"Two o'clock," a gunner called as another enemy Menacer Mark I began firing at them.

Rommond turned the Hopebreaker and made straight for the enemy landship, which began to flee, but a single shell from the turret stopped it straight in its tracks, adding another warning to the armoured forces that guarded the Hope factory.

The Hopebreaker rolled into the factory complex, followed by several slower and less advanced landships from the Resistance's armoured arsenal. Behemoths could not operate in those narrow streets, but the Regime had many other vehicles there, none of which were any match for the Hopebreaker. Rommond drove down alleys, destroying Moving Castles and Menacer Mark I's as he went, until there were few Regime landships left, and they were quickly hunted down by the rest of Rommond's army.

Then Rommond drove the Hopebreaker straight through the walls of the factory itself, and the bricks crumbled down around the vehicle, battering off the hull like a new type of rain. It did not take many shells to destroy the machinery inside, and Rommond paid little attention to the slaves, many of whom died in the gunfire, and some of whom still tried to work on broken conveyor belts.

"I don't see Taberah," Lieutenant Tradam said.

"We'll find them," Rommond replied. He had not given up hope just yet.

Chapter Seventeen

MISSION: ALONE

Had Jacob not seen the Hopebreaker approaching, he would have still known it was outside, for the booming of its turret gun was like thunder from an angry god, and he thought that Rommond must have been very angry.

Taberah led them through the maze of corridors, up flights of stairs, and across platforms, always ducking low as they went, as if the very ceiling were trying to get them. Jacob noticed that she used her shotgun for support as she moved, and at times he tried to help her, but she shrugged him off, and he thought that she might have even fired upon him to prove she did not need any help.

Jacob did not know where in the factory he was, and it seemed that Taberah did not know either. Everything looked the same to him, and when he thought they might be passing by the same production hall, he noticed that the slaves inside were different in face and feature, but always the same in their lifeless expressions and their methodical working. At times he had to be dragged away from those halls, for he felt compelled to do something about them, but felt as equally helpless.

Taberah halted them suddenly when the sound of voices came from up ahead. They were gruff and severe, and Jacob could only imagine that they must belong to the mouths of Regime soldiers. Taberah readied her gun, and the others followed suit.

As soon as the guards appeared at the bottom of the stairs ahead of them, they were gunned down in seconds. Jacob liked the feel of his rifle; he did not like the sight of what it could do.

Taberah led them up the stairs, and she fired her shotgun and reloaded as she ran, killing several guards in her way. Jacob and the others followed quickly behind her, firing on small groups of soldiers that appeared down corridors or across the way on the ramparts.

Jacob began to wonder if instead of leading them out of the winding complex, Taberah was leading them further inside. It did not look like she was trying to escape. It looked like she was trying to hunt someone down. *Domas*, Jacob thought. He could think of no one better to die by Taberah's shotgun.

They barged through the doors of a large storage chamber and stumbled into a contingent of Regime soldiers, hurriedly looting a box of grenades for use against the landships outside. Taberah fired at them before even considering the risk of the grenades going off with all of them inside.

One of the soldiers used his final crumb of will to pull the pin out of one of the grenades, and his final ounce of strength to cast it towards them.

"Out!" Jacob cried, and they charged out with him before the entire room blew up and coughed out a viscous plume of smoke.

With those grenades gone, perhaps Rommond would be as thankful to them as they were to him. Yet against the armour of the Hopebreaker, Jacob thought that perhaps not even a full box of grenades would do.

As the dust began to clear, Jacob realised that he was alone. He had thrown himself in one direction, while the others had cast themselves to the opposing side. That was his hope, at least, for he did not like the idea that they were thrown by the grenades instead.

He waited longer than he ought to, expecting another explosion, visualising another grenade rolling out the door to greet him. The smoke took ages to diffuse, and even when it did, there was dust in his eyes. He was just glad there was not debris in his skin.

"Taberah," he whispered. He crawled quickly past the ruined room and peeped around a corner, but found no one there. In this place, if there were to be anyone there, chances are it would be a Regime soldier. He was every bit a gambler, but he did not like these odds.

He decided against calling her name again. *I might as well call for the Iron Emperor*, he thought, *for all the good that making a racket in here would do.*

He stopped for a moment and took stock of where he was. It looked like the fourth floor, and he could see down into one of the production chambers, where those chainless slaves continued to be oblivious to him and their surroundings, and their potential freedom. He looked right and left, but he could not see a stairwell down. There were stairs up to a higher level, but he did not think that would help him get out of this place any quicker.

You're on your own, Taberah, he thought. *So am I.* It was useful to recognise this. It meant he could readjust his priorities, focus on smuggling himself out. It was easier to look after just one person. At least if he stumbled or failed, he would know who to blame.

He decided to go left, where he heard the most explosions outside. In any other situation he would have run in the opposite direction, but chances were that these explosions were caused by Rommond's army. He liked those odds.

He followed the platform around the production chamber until he found a door. He opened it carefully and peeked into the darkness inside. When in the house of the enemy, the best rooms are always the ones with the lights out. He listened to the shadow inside to see if it stirred, but all he could hear was the booming outside.

Suddenly he heard the sound of footsteps in the chamber down below. He saw a contingent of guards walking through, led by Domas. He hoped to all gods, and all devils, that Taberah was in pursuit, and part of him even felt like taking a shot at the general from here, despite the likelihood that he would die in the process.

"I want that landship," Domas barked. "Functioning or destroyed."

"Aye, sir."

"Don't *aye* me. Make it happen."

Just as Domas cast a glance up, Jacob crept into

the dark room and waited for the guards below to leave. As his eyes adjusted to the gloom, he realised he was in a filing room, with many documents and maps on show. In the game of war there were many ways to hit the jackpot. This was one of them.

He bundled up as many of the documents he could handle, stuffing them into his belt. He thought they might be useful to the Resistance, and that he might even be able to sell them. He hoped they were worth the risk, because every time he moved, they crinkled and rubbed against one another, causing what sounded to his ears like cries for help. They were hostages he could not silence, and he knew that taking them made the odds of his escape even lower.

When he could no longer hear Domas and his men, he sneaked outside and crept along the platform, cursing the stolen papers with every step. He continued to open and close doors carefully as he went, looking for any that might lead downstairs. All of them seemed to be storage rooms, and perhaps more of them had useful documents, but he decided he had taken enough prisoners.

He had to make his way around almost the entirety of the production chamber before he found a way down. He rolled his eyes at the thought that he would have found it quicker if he had gone right instead.

He continued to hear the booming of the Hope-breaker outside as he crept down the metal stairs. He wished it were wood instead. His boots made little explosions of their own upon those steps. He alternated between grimacing and holding his breath as he descended, and his fingers pawed his rifle for reassurance.

When he reached the last step, he peeked down the corridor on either side and saw no one, and heard no one. When trying to escape, it was good to feel alone. He decided to stick with the left path, for fear that fate would enjoy him changing his mind, and he stalked down the empty corridor, hugging the wall, hiding in his own shadow.

At the end of this path was a closed door, behind which was the clear glimmer of an oil lamp. Jacob was faced with a choice, a gamble, like red or black. He could go back and take the right path, and perhaps find a room with no one inside, or he could take a chance and storm the one he stood in front of. He did not like giving fate an advantage, but fate knew well that he was a betting man.

He gripped the handle of the door and took a deep breath. Then suddenly the handle turned, as if by its own accord. The door opened inwards, and Jacob stood face to face with a stunned guard. There was a moment of pause for both of them as they stood shocked, and it might have only been half a second, but in that time Jacob could see every line, every crack, every shadow upon the guard's bewildered face.

Then the half a second was up, and the struggle began. Jacob tried to shove his rifle forward, but the guard was too close, and he seized it and pushed Jacob back. Jacob almost tripped, but he managed to jam his foot in time and push back. Both of them were now firmly gripping the rifle, which was held horizontally before them, and each of them used it to push the other back. The guard was stronger than Jacob, but luckily he was not as big as some of the other ones, or the fight would have ended much more quickly, and the gamble would have ended with a payout of Jacob's blood. He pushed Jacob back against the wall of the corridor, forcing a groan from him as his back smacked off the wall. The pain fuelled his own strength, and he did the same to the guard against the other wall. Then they swung around and stumbled into the gas-lit room, where they continued to push each other against the walls, as if the very bricks were their attackers.

Jacob did not like this tug of war. For each inch gained, it was lost again in moments. The stolen papers crinkled and crunched as he moved, as if in wild applause. He knew with grim certainty that they were not cheering for him.

The guard shoved him towards a table, and Jacob felt the edge strike his back. He yelped in pain, and then he saw new shadows thrown against the walls, as if they too were having their own tug of war. He realised that the gas lamp on the table had been knocked over, and he felt the flames behind him, and he saw the flickering light from the corner of his eyes.

This was a useful distraction that helped Jacob cast the guard back to the floor. He pointed the rifle and prepared to click the trigger. But then the fire exploded behind him, and he was knocked forward on top of the guard, who immediately seized the gun again. It fired as he fell, blowing a hole in the wall, and in the dancing shadows upon it.

Jacob rolled around on the floor with the guard, pushing and shoving. He tried to use his knees or elbows to subdue his attacker, but the guard struck back with just as much ferocity. In such a fight he thought he might be able to feel the demon in the man become more apparent, but his struggle seemed altogether human. To win this battle Jacob thought he might have to instead find the demon in himself.

Just when he thought he had the edge, just as he was forcing the rifle against the guard's throat, the flaming oil crept up beside him and forced him to stop. He tried to roll away, but the guard still gripped the gun, and both of them were only forced to let it go when the fire exploded once more, sending the rifle into the corner of the room.

Jacob fell upon his bruised back, and he gave a loud moan, but the desire to live won the struggle against his pain, and he forced himself up and tried to clamber over to the gun. He was too late, however, for the guard got there first. He stood pointing the rifle at him, but he did not fire.

"Back away!" the man cried, his voice as bruised as his body.

Jacob stepped back and raised his hands. He thought of charging at the man, at making one last ditch effort to subdue him, even if it meant he would die in the process. It was better than dying with his hands up. Yet living was better still.

"Turn around!" the guard ordered. It was an uncertain order, as if he was more used to receiving them than giving them.

Jacob reluctantly complied. He liked even less the

idea of dying with his back turned. He felt the butt of the gun in his battered back, and he grimaced from the pain, and his bruised pride grimaced even more.

"Go!" the guard said. "Walk!"

Jacob walked straight ahead, out the door on the opposite side he had come in from. The corridor was lit more brightly here, but there was still no one else in sight. He hoped now that Taberah might stumble by, that he might now end this mission alone.

He continued on, down a flight of stairs and around several bends, led by the butt of the gun, which carved directions in his spine. He could hear and feel the heavy breathing of the guard behind him, and he could sense the nervousness in those breaths.

They passed another production chamber, and Jacob slowed as they went. More slaves were there, wasting away as they produced the very thing that would stop the demons following suit.

"That's why we fight you," Jacob said, pointing into the chamber.

The gun pushed him on.

"As long as there's evil like you," Jacob said, "there'll always be people like us who'll fight."

"We're not all like that," the guard said with hesitation.

"I'll believe you when I no longer feel the barrel of a gun in my back."

"We didn't ask for this," the guard said.

"Well, you got it all the same."

"I'm just doing my job."

"That doesn't absolve you from your crime."

"I have a family to feed."

"Whole families are dying in there!" Jacob said, pointing back towards the production chamber.

"I want to help," the guard said, "but there's nothing I can do."

Jacob shook his head violently. "Stop being a cog in the machine."

The guard did not answer, but Jacob could hear more hesitation in his breathing. They passed down another two flights of stairs and approached a door that led out into the street.

"Keep going!" the guard said.

"You know, it's probably not safe outside," Jacob said. He could still hear the booming, though it had grown a little fainter. He hoped that meant there were few enemy vehicles left to destroy.

When they were outside, Jacob was amazed at the sight. There were fires and ruins everywhere, and he could not see very far with all the dust and smoke. Yet they were barely outside a few minutes when he heard the revving of an engine and saw something approaching through the haze.

The Hopebreaker rolled up and halted before Jacob and the quivering Regime guard, whose hands might have shook even more were they not gripping the rifle tightly. A plume of dust rose between the armoured transport and the two small men who stood before it. When it died down, there was a moment of intense silence and stillness, where nothing seemed to move, and no one dared to make a sound.

"Back away!" the Regime soldier cried to the landship, as if it were a metal monster that could be reasoned with, as if it might baulk at his command.

But the monster did not quiver, and the monster did not answer, and the monster did not back away.

Suddenly the hatch on the top of the Hopebreaker swung open with a clang, and Rommond stood up waist high from it. He barely glanced about before grabbing his pistol and firing once at the soldier holding Jacob, who collapsed upon the ground holding closed the wound.

"Good hit," Jacob said.

Rommond smiled wryly. "Maybe I missed."

Chapter Eighteen

WRECKAGE

When they had left the grounds of the Hope factory and were about a mile away, Rommond stopped the landship and got out, followed by the others. He grabbed the binoculars off one of his crewmen and stared through them at the ruin he had created. He stared for a long time, longer than Jacob thought was necessary. *What could there really be to see?* he thought. *A ruin is a ruin.*

"That factory will take at least five years to rebuild," Rommond said, but he did not sound proud. Taberah could not contain her grin, and she had pride enough for all of them. The Order had made many sacrifices, but through their efforts, so had the Regime.

"Let's hope the Regime won't be here in five years," she said.

Rommond continued to stare through the binoculars, as if he was continuing his bombardment of the factory with his eyes. "Let's hope," he said, with not a hint of enthusiasm.

"For a man who just won a major battle, you don't sound that chuffed about it," Jacob said.

Rommond's gaze did not falter. "It was too easy."

Jacob laughed. "You have an odd definition of

easy."

Taberah rubbed Rommond's left shoulder, like she might have done had he lost the battle. "Come on, Rommond, can't we celebrate these little wins?"

"While we celebrate, the Regime will be planning its counterattack," Rommond predicted. "We cannot allow ourselves to be caught unprepared." He held out the binoculars to his side, and the crewman rushed up to take them.

Rommond turned to Taberah. "We all need to lay low for a while."

"Not exactly my favourite pastime," Taberah said. She looked as though she was eager to move on to the next Hope factory, to starve the Regime into oblivion.

"I know, but it's important you don't draw too much attention. And you," Rommond added, turning to Jacob. "You should lay low as well."

"Don't worry," Jacob replied. "I don't have a problem with that at all."

Rommond's sight was seized by the ruins once more. None of them needed binoculars to see the plumes of smoke. At one time they were the signs of industry. Now they were the signs of war.

"I didn't want to play my hand this early," Rommond said, "and I'd rather the Regime not raise the stakes. But its people will demand retribution, and the Iron Emperor will be all too willing to meet that demand."

"They can't hurt us if they don't know where we are," Taberah said. "We can hide in Dustdelving."

Rommond did not seem so confident. "They will be looking for us with greater vigour than before.

Now they know for certain that I am still alive. We will have to be extra careful, or all that we have built over the last three years will be destroyed."

"Maybe this'll cheer you up," Jacob said. "I got you something." He held out the bunch of documents, badly damaged from his fight.

"You shouldn't have," Rommond replied.

"I do my bit."

"So it seems," the general said as he flicked quickly through the papers. "Unfortunately, most of these are worthless."

"Well, I wasn't going to charge."

"Good," Rommond replied. "I wasn't going to pay."

Jacob gave a smirk. He liked this repartee. It was like a friendly gunfight. No one really got hurt.

"So," Jacob said, and he knocked upon the hull of the Hopebreaker, much to Rommond's annoyance. *Perhaps he believes I'll scratch the paint*, Jacob thought. The green stood out starkly against the red sands. *It could do with scratching.*

"Yes?" Rommond asked impatiently.

"Why didn't you paint it red like the other landships? It would blend in better."

"I don't want it to blend in," Rommond explained. "I want it to stand out. I want the Regime to see this from a mile away and tremble at its coming, and collapse at its arrival. This is the Hopebreaker. For every shell it fires at a physical target, let there be another that strikes their hearts."

"Fair enough," Jacob said. "I guess you really hate them."

Rommond turned his gaze upon him, as if it were the crosshairs of a rifle. "More than you know," he said, and behind the sternness of his voice there was a shackled anger, and beneath that shackled anger there was a buried pain. Jacob decided not to ask any more.

Taberah kissed Rommond on the cheek, the kind of kiss of a mother wishing her soldier son will come home again. He did not kiss her back; his eyes were still set on the smoulder of the Hope factory, as if it were an omen. Though the smoke billowed far away, it cast an evil shadow on his face.

"I will wait here until your warwagon arrives," Rommond said. He ordered his soldiers to remain alert. Jacob could not help but feel alert as well.

As Rommond began to look through the stolen Regime documents in more detail, and periodically look in all directions for attackers, Jacob took Taberah aside.

"I guess this is where we part ways," Jacob said. He was glad that all of this was over, but he could not help feel just a hint of sadness.

"I guess," Taberah replied.

"At least you got me to go on one last mission."

"There is that."

Jacob felt a little awkward, like he had to explain himself to her. The more jobs he did for the Order, the harder it seemed to quit. It was like an addiction. He wondered if Taberah was his drug pusher.

"I couldn't by any chance get a lift?" Jacob asked. "I don't fancy the walk back to Blackout."

"Are you sure you want to go back to such a populated city?"

"I'm good at hiding in a crowd."

"You stand out enough to me."

Taberah's warwagon pulled up. While it looked advanced when Jacob saw it first, it seemed rather quaint and dated now that it stood beside the Hopebreaker. Part of him wished that Rommond would drop him off instead.

"It's been nice knowing you," Jacob said to the Resistance soldiers. "Good luck with the war."

Rommond gave the slightest of nods. Perhaps it simply meant *Farewell*, or perhaps instead it was a grimmer greeting: *Good luck with your own war.*

The warwagon seemed more cramped than it did before. The corridors were crushingly close, and the rooms were claustrophobically small. Jacob was thankful that Blackout was so near, and yet a part of him would not have minded a longer journey. He was particularly sad that he did not get to say goodbye to Whistler. *He'll be fine*, he told himself.

It was not long before they stopped outside Blackout, at that familiar distance outside the gaze of the guards.

"I guess this is my stop," Jacob said. He got up and stood beside the door.

"Aren't you forgetting something?" Taberah asked.

"What, do you want a goodbye kiss?"

Taberah laughed. "No. Your money. Your crate of coils."

"Mind it for me," Jacob said. "I'll be back for it." As he said it, he wondered if he was giving himself an excuse to go back for her.

"I'll spend it for you," Taberah joked.

"You wouldn't dare."

He waved and hopped out of the warwagon. He decided to walk towards a crowd of traders who had gathered outside the city and enter with them. In a way, smuggling was its own kind of trade.

Jacob entered Blackout just as the stars were coming out, like little spies watching his movements through the shadows. The city was very quiet. He half expected the Regime to be out in force, but it was likely that they were scouring the desert instead. They knew the Hope factory's destruction was the work of the Resistance, and they knew that few in Blackout would resist them.

Jacob followed the back alleys, over the homeless, into *The Olive Inn*, a small tavern known for its cheap prices, average beer, and loud landlord.

"Your rent is overdue," the landlord Gus said as soon as he had entered, as if he was waiting there night and day for him to return.

Jacob flicked a coil over to him, which he caught with ease.

"This isn't enough," Gus stated.

"Trust me," Jacob said. "You'll get the rest, with interest, soon."

"I've been trusting you for a very long time."

"Then trust me a little longer."

"You pay your rent and you'll buy my trust."

Jacob ran up the stairs, skipping several steps,

and he heard the shouts and threats of the landlord run after him. They were empty threats, like a parent threatening to cast out a child. It was part of what he liked about this place.

Like the warwagon, his room seemed a little quainter than it did before. He might have thought differently had he returned to it straight from the Hold. He was never quite content in this tiny hovel, which was far too expensive for what it was, but he felt less content in it now than he had before. This was the old life he was trying to get back to. This was what he was trying to get away from the Order for.

The grass is always greener, he thought. *The sands are always redder*, he corrected.

He lit the oil lamp in the room, noting that the oil was low, and that the landlord would not be so happy to top it up. With that crate of coils, he could buy every room in the building. Hell, he could buy the entire inn. But he could not exactly haul the crate into Blackout without being noticed. He would have to smuggle in a handful of coils each time. It would be like a new kind of job, but one that was prepaid.

The lamp highlighted his small bookcase, with less than a dozen books. He took one of them up called *The Essential Guide to Minerals*, and he opened it to reveal a cavity in which was placed two amulets. He would not exactly need them any more, and yet part of him felt like continuing where he had left off, just for that little thrill, for that sense of defying the Regime. It was his own little war.

When Jacob placed the book back, he noticed a slip of paper wedged in another tome. He knew for certain he did not place it there himself. He took it out slowly, feeling the richness of the paper, and he looked with wonder upon the large printed letters that clearly showed it was not the product of the working class, who did not have access to printing presses. He was transfixed by the offer it made:

TO WHOM IT MAY CONCERN

We, patrons of good fortune and a most estimable sort, invite you to consider a limited time proposal, made only to a handful of ladies and gentlemen throughout Blackout, all judged to be of good society.

We guarantee that all who take up this offer shall be rewarded handsomely, and that though it never rains upon the sands of Blackout, it shall always rain coils upon the heads of all good folk who avail of this notice.

The work we require is small, but the rewards are large. We, a most noble caste of benefactors, believe it is our duty to share our enormous wealth with those who would make good use of it, and have carefully selected those who, in our discerning eyes, should be the beneficiaries of said wealth.

If you, good sir or madam, should like to take up this offer, we would be delighted to share your good company, and you our good fortune, at the circus tent of the recently returned fairground, which is as fleeting as this one time offer.

Inform no one. Come alone.

Jacob scoffed as he read, but even as doubt rose with each paragraph, another emotion stirred, and he began to question his own doubts, and he began to wonder if passing up this offer, as he was first inclined to do, might be a grave mistake, and he might forever regret the missed opportunity, and rue a fortune he might squander in a far better way.

Though it sounded too good to be true, he could not entirely dismiss the offer. After all, it was following the instructions in a random note like this that got him started smuggling amulets into Blackout in the first place.

He went back and forth on this all night, until he could no longer find his fortune of sleep. He stirred in the pitch of darkness, and he paced restlessly to and fro before his bed, and before the lonely bookcase on which the notice sat like an idol. The night gave him no answers, and when dawn finally came, he realised that the day gave none either.

Yet Jacob was allured by the offer, and he preferred not to be an informer, and he preferred not to work with others. So he informed no one, and he went to the fairground alone.

Chapter Nineteen

FORTUNE-TELLER

Jacob had not been to a fairground since he was a child. The rides just did not thrill him any more. The sense of danger was not as good as the one he got when smuggling amulets in or out of the city, where the thrill was not the crank of a roller-coaster, but the click of a gun.

The fair opened twice a year, and some saw it as the greatest triumph of entertainment, of the amusing and fun, and some saw it as the greatest expression of artistry, of the strange and bizarre, but Jacob saw it for what it really was: a distraction. Its arrival coincided with that of the Regime's rise to power, and some heralded it as an example of the government's respect for the people, while Jacob knew that it only served to disguise the Regime's true efforts to make the entire world its fairground.

There were children present, but they were not human children, even if to a casual eye they looked exactly the same. They ran and played and laughed like Jacob had when he was young, but he knew that they were different, and that by the time those children were old, the human race might cease to exist.

Here and there Jacob saw people putting up large posters, which depicted the destruction of the nearby Hope factory. The posters had many different slogans, the kind of things the Regime had been putting on posters for years:

THE RESISTANCE HAS BROUGHT YOU
A GIFT: FAMINE.

WE OFFER HOPE. THEY DESTROY IT.

AND THEY CALL *US* MONSTERS.

Already there were many people gathering around them, growing more incensed by the second. Words and images were very powerful weapons. Jacob decided to stay far away from those people who had just been armed.

Jacob continued on, trying to appear at least a little amused by the attractions.

Suddenly he noticed a contingent of Regime guards across the way, circulating posters of various criminals accused of all manner of depravity. He had a dark suspicion that his face and name might be among them. He was curious as to what evil things they might have claimed of him, just as they had with Teller and so many others in the Order, but he was not curious enough to find out.

He looked around for somewhere to hide. His dark brown attire almost stood out against the backdrop of primary red, yellow and blue. His dour expression certainly stood out amidst all the smiles and happy faces.

He saw a small tent labelled Madame Mavilio, dotted with stars and moons, as if it were an invocation of the night. He ducked inside it as the guards passed. He could hear their heavy boots above the monotonous fairground music, creating a monotony of their own. He could almost hear his heart following suit.

He barely noticed the old lady inside, hovering her hands over a crystal ball like the many blimps and dirigibles hovered over the city of Blackout.

"Your fortune for a coil, sir," she said, holding out her wrinkled palm, wrinkled perhaps by clutching many coils seized from the pockets of the unwary and unquestioning.

"I don't have a coil to spare," Jacob whispered.

"This is for customers only," the Madame explained, but still she held her hand out, as if she foresaw his future as a customer.

Jacob grumbled as he pulled a solitary coil from his pocket. He never liked having just one, because it meant there was no chink as it clashed against another. That was the only kind of music he liked to hear.

He reluctantly handed the coil to the palm reader, whose own fortune got that little bit more plentiful. She cast it into a box beneath the table, and he heard that familiar, reassuring clink.

"Your palm," she said.

Jacob slowly showed her the palm of his right hand.

"Don't be shy," she said, and she pulled his hand

closer. "The future is nothing to be afraid of." Jacob begged to differ. Those who lived before the time of the Harvest had no idea what evil future awaited them. Jacob did not want to know what awaited him, did not want to dwell on the idea that his present might be sowing the seeds of an even greater reaping.

"I see a troubled past," the old lady explained, focusing on one of the lines that ran across his palm like rivers. Perhaps she saw diverging waters. Perhaps she saw a dam.

I see a con artist, Jacob thought. *Maybe this is what I should have done for a living.* His mind reminded him of the chink in the box beneath the table. He began to wonder just how many coils it contained.

The old woman eyed him quickly to see his reaction. "Very troubled," she continued. "Lots of moving from place to place. Always restless. Never settling. You work in transport, I presume."

You're the fortune-teller, Jacob thought. *You shouldn't have to presume anything.* "Yes," he said reluctantly, as if his answer were another coil parting from his pocket.

"I see something big on the horizon. A fortune."

Jacob had to struggle to prevent him rolling his eyes. He wondered how many hundreds, perhaps even thousands, of people she had said that to, how many eager ears had heard her promises, and how many hopeful hearts had believed them. Yet for Jacob, there was perhaps some truth that she was not aware of, and he began to wonder for a moment if she was part of that elite caste the notice had spoken of.

"A great fortune," the woman said, stressing

just how great it was by widening her eyes, as if the mountain of coils she saw in the spirit world was immensely shocking.

"Sounds nice," Jacob said, indulging her, even as she would indulge herself in her own wealth, accumulated at the expense of the gullible. "How will I come upon it?"

"I'm getting to that," the Madame said irritably, and she gently tapped his hand in remonstration for breaking her concentration and interrupting her solemn ritual. "Give me my due time and I'll get to it."

Jacob listened to the sounds outside. He did not hear the march of boots. "Thanks, but I have to go," he said, pulling his hand away.

The Madame almost came with it. "But your fortune," she stammered.

"I'll see what it is with my own two eyes."

He crept outside and hurried onwards towards the large circus tent, which towered above the other attractions. The circus only opened at night, but some of the acts were wandering around the fairground as if they had nothing else to do.

He passed by the various freaks on display: a bearded lady, a two-headed creature, and a man who was half machine, with pistons where an arm should be, and cogs where an eye should be. A crowd surrounded these unsettling sideshows, casting condemning fingers and judgemental glances. Yet Jacob wondered if they even knew that some who walked among them were even greater freaks, not of nature, but of a demonic world that none of them knew anything about.

Jacob entered the circus tent, which was dim and eerily quiet. He had not been to a circus since he was a child, and though he found it a bewildering experience then, he found the emptiness inside this great canopy even more unsettling.

Yet the tent was not altogether empty, for soon he found he was bumping into and tripping over crates by the dozen. As he regained his footing, his eyes settled on what looked for a moment like a familiar figure. He blinked and strained his sight, and the image did not dissipate. It was Teller.

"Looking for a new line of work?" Jacob asked. "I didn't take you for a carny."

"I am here to offer *you* a new line of work," Teller said.

"I don't think I'd make a great tightrope walker."

"But you make a good clown," Teller remarked, and he adjusted his glasses, as if to see Jacob's makeup.

Jacob stumbled into another crate of coils. They were everywhere. Under any other circumstances, he would have been delighted. With Teller there, he thought that every box must have had a greasy handle.

"What's this?" Jacob asked, but really he was asking why.

"Fifty thousand coils," Teller said, rubbing his hands together, as if they were all his. "A fortune."

"Who's fortune?"

"Yours, if you want it."

Of course I want it, Jacob thought. *Who wouldn't?* Even Rommond would kill to have this kind of funding. Perhaps he already had.

"That's a lot of money to smuggle amulets," Jacob said.

"It is not about amulets, but rather Edward Rommond."

"I'm not following," Jacob said. "Why would Taberah offer me all this money when she didn't even like me taking my rightful cut before? And she has her own route to Rommond."

"This offer does not come from her," Teller revealed. "It comes from the Regime."

Jacob was dumbstruck. He instinctively looked around for Regime guards, but it was so dark inside the tent that he could not see any. He felt like running, but the coils told him to stay.

"So you posed for that poster yourself," Jacob said, gritting his teeth. "No wonder you are so proud of it. And no wonder Rommond never liked you. He must have had a feeling."

"Feelings are irrelevant if they are not acted on," Teller said. "So much for his famed tactics."

"He destroyed the Hope factory, didn't he?"

"One of them, yes, and that is why we are here," Teller acknowledged. "We want to know where Rommond's base is."

"Well, I don't know where it is."

"Liar!" Teller growled, and his hands instinctively reached out, as if to choke him. "You have *been* there. You should know the way."

"It doesn't work like that," Jacob explained. "They didn't show me the way. It was all twists and turns. I honestly haven't a clue."

Teller adjusted his glasses again, as if to see

through Jacob's lies. "I do not believe you."

"Then don't. It doesn't matter to me."

"It will," Teller said ominously.

"You've been in Taberah's camp long enough," Jacob said. "Why didn't you get her to tell you?"

"I have never gotten as close to her as you have." He almost seemed personally wounded, as if this was more than just vengeance for the Regime.

"Maybe you're not so persuasive."

"With her, no, but with you, perhaps I am persuasive enough."

"I don't think so," Jacob said, but he was cut short by Teller kicking one of the open crates over to him. He felt his heart jump a little, and his eyes fixed on the coils inside.

Teller smiled. "Or maybe the money is all the persuasion I need."

It took a great effort on Jacob's part to reef his eyes from those coils, and even when he no longer looked at them, he felt almost like they were looking at him, into his very heart and soul. He let out a terrible sigh, as if it were the demon of greed that had possessed him.

"Unlike you," Jacob said coldly, "I don't betray my friends."

"They're nothing to you," Teller said. "A few weeks ago you never even knew them. You have a chance to retire on a massive fortune, to live out your days in wealth and luxury. No more smuggling, no more trying to earn a quick buck. And we'll forget about your record, and you can forget about us and this Order business."

"It isn't all about the money," Jacob said.

Teller kicked another crate over, and Jacob's heart fluttered once more.

"Isn't it?" Teller asked.

"Maybe I like the odd jobs. Maybe I like the thrills."

"You can buy fifty thousand thrills with this."

"You can't buy thrills," Jacob said.

"You disappoint me, Jacob," Teller said, fidgeting with his hands again. "I pegged you for a business man. However, if money will not persuade you, then perhaps this will."

A spotlight came on in the centre of the tent. Each night it would illuminate the ringmaster, but now it showed Whistler tied to a chair, surrounded by several guards. His mouth was gagged, his hair was a mess, and he had many bruises on his face and arms. He looked like he had put up a fight, and even now it seemed like he was trying to shout and scream through the tape across his mouth. He was clearly as defiant as Jacob, perhaps emboldened by him, but his eyes showed that he was just as worried as Jacob was. Defiance stands in the face of fear; it does not conquer it.

"Whistler," Teller said, rolling the name around on his tongue. "You know, I always liked that name, much better than the one Taberah gave to him. So much for what it means, however. He did not blow the whistle on me. Of course, he could have been called Crier or Wailer once we dragged him here. And, as you can see, he can't exactly whistle right now."

"What do you want?" Jacob asked, clenching his

fists.

"I already told you. I want to know the way to Dustdelving."

Jacob took a deep breath and sighed. "Rommond lives in the bowels of the earth, in the gusts of the wind, and in the stars in the sky."

"How droll," Teller said. "Three wrong directions." He struck Whistler three times upon the face. Though he was gagged, his muffled cries could still be heard. "You are not hurting me," Teller continued. "You are hurting him."

Jacob tried to disguise his concern. "What makes you think I care about him? I'm a smuggler. I do things my way. I fight for my side, no one else's."

"I do not care what you are, Jacob, so long as you are a guide to Dustdelving." He held his hand up above Whistler. "Be careful with your next words, lest they be a guide for my hand to his face."

"Okay, okay. I lied before. I do know the way. Dustdelving is three lefts and one right on the Worn Road from Copperfort."

"Good try, Jacob, but I do not just want directions. I want you to take me there."

"And if I don't?"

"You already know the answer to that question, Jacob," Teller said. "If you do not show us the way to Rommond's hideout, then poor little Whistler here will die."

Chapter Twenty

DELVING FOR DUST

Jacob was ushered into an armoured carrier at gun point. It seemed that Teller did not trust him, because Jacob saw the points of many guns, and the stern glances of many soldiers.

"A bit overkill, don't you think?"

"For you, it is just enough," Teller said, with a hint of scorn.

Jacob wanted to say, *For me, it is not enough,* but he knew that it was not true. The brutal reality of the world was that it only took a single bullet, and in Altadas that bullet could come from anywhere, from friendly fire or enemy onslaught. If this was a game of death, he was currently winning.

Whistler was also dragged on board, still gagged and bound, and he squirmed all the time, making it difficult for the soldiers trying to fasten him into one of the seats. He might have been small and frail, but he had some fight in him, and Jacob thought that it was almost admirable.

"Jacob," Teller said, "tell the boy to stop fighting or we will have to fight back."

Jacob hoped not to have to look at Whistler's bruised face. It was too much of a distraction. He turned around and pleaded with his eyes as much as his voice. "Just relax," he said. "There's no point fighting." He tried to communicate something more with his eyes: *There's no point fighting now.*

"You will prove useful after all," Teller said as Whistler quietened down.

Jacob smirked. "I'll send you my bill."

"You already refused fifty thousand coils."

"Maybe I charge more than that."

"If you get us to Dustdelving, you can name any price, and we will pay."

Jacob looked anxiously out at the desert. *If I get us to Dustdelving, we all will pay.*

The carrier started up, jolting forward. It was a very different feeling to the Hopebreaker, which glided smoothly across the sand. He wondered if the Regime in some way enjoyed these bumpy rides, or if they simply did not have the engineering skills of Rommond's team. He was tempted to make some remark about the vehicle's sluggishness, and he might have done if Whistler was not there to receive a beating.

He thought for a moment about trying to remember the twists and turns to Dustdelving, but it was all a blur. He knew for certain that they headed south, which was why he opted to lead the Regime north instead. He hoped his ploy was not that obvious. He was never so happy to be a good liar.

They began the long journey north towards Copperfort, the last true refuge of humanity, largely left alone by the Regime, thanks to the constant sorties and skirmishes of various tribes in the area to the east, and perhaps the Regime's own desire to keep just enough human women alive to act as portals for their demon offspring, until their old domain was empty.

As they drove, Jacob racked his brains for some kind of plan, but the imposing presence of the guards, and the slimy presence of Teller, made it difficult to think. Whistler's presence could barely be felt. He hoped it was because Whistler was better at hiding than Jacob was, not because his life was ebbing away. *It might not matter in the end*, Jacob thought, *not if I can't figure something out before they figure me out.* The problem with lies was that the truth always got in the way.

The journey crawled in, giving Jacob plenty of time to think, but he almost wished it would go in faster, that it would all be over with, but Whistler's worried glances gave him a new inner strength, just as Whistler's encouraging words did in the Hold.

Jacob felt Teller's probing glare penetrating him. Perhaps he could see through the metal walls of the armoured carrier. Jacob was almost certain that Teller could see into his soul. He was glad he did not hide his lies there.

"This is quite an adventure you have had," Teller said.

"Envy doesn't become you, Teller."

Teller held his breath for a second and tapped his fingers upon the side of his chair. "Your tongue has a mind of its own."

"At least there's two between us then."

Teller forced a laugh; it echoed in the vehicle, as

if it were bouncing off every wall. "How droll," Teller said at last, as if he could not think of anything else to say.

"So what are you, exactly?" Jacob asked.

"Hmm?"

"What are you? A spy? A gun-for-hire? Did you ever really belong to the Order, or is this all some kind of retribution against Rommond?"

"Why does it matter?"

"Call it curiosity."

"I am just doing my duty," Teller said, with that same kind of pride he displayed when standing beside his famous poster, "serving the Iron Emperor in any way I can."

"So a spy then."

"If you want, yes."

"No, I want you to admit it."

"Why?"

"I want your conscience to hear it."

"What makes you think I have a conscience?"

"Everybody has one."

"Every human has one," Teller corrected.

This was what Jacob hated most about the demons. They looked like everybody else. It was why the Order needed someone like Whistler. It was why his failure to detect some demons was such a grievous blow.

"So, the posters of you, condemning you for your deeds for the Order. They were all a lie."

"They were rather convincing," Teller said, and he beamed, as if he had come up with the idea himself. "I almost believed them myself."

"Do you regularly believe your own lies?"

Teller tilted his head. "Do you?"

Throughout this exchange, the soldiers kept a level gaze straight ahead, while Whistler stared at the ceiling of the carrier, as if he was trying to drown out the verbal dispute, like a child who does not want to hear his parents arguing.

Silence fell with night, but Jacob could not entirely quieten his racing mind, nor speed it up to the finish line. He felt no closer to a solution to their problem. He was sure he could save Dustdelving, but he was not sure he could save Whistler or himself.

He slept uneasily that night, and he was not entirely sure he slept at all. He thought perhaps he was having a nightmare, but he soon realised the nightmare was when he was wide awake. Teller was a monster in his sleep, a mangled, twisted form, something he could see, something he could fear, something he could condemn. The reality was much more frightening.

Then he heard his wake-up call.

"We are here," Teller said. He looked very human, but he was still a monster.

Jacob sat up, feeling panic sweep through him. He was out of time. The miserly night brought very little sleep, and no solutions. It shared nothing with them, keeping every crumb of light to itself.

"Where are we?" Jacob asked when he looked out. The desert mocked the map-makers. Yet when it came to entering the Regime's territory, flying bullets were often as good as any compass. No bullets flew that day.

"Just north of Copperfort," Teller told him. "Now it is your turn to drive."

They handed him the steering sticks. He wished instead they handed him a gun. He did not like the idea of driving to his own death, to his own ruin. Yet even as his hands grasped the steering sticks, he felt a surge of confidence flow through him, and he began to formulate a plan.

"Drive us straight to Dustdelving," Teller ordered.

"Sure. You might need more than these few soldiers to storm that place though."

"This is not a raiding party, Jacob. We are the scouts, if you will." Teller produced a small device with a blinking red light. Jacob thought it was a bomb.

"This is a tracker," Teller said. "When we go in to get Rommond, we will be sending an army. He will not get away this time."

Jacob tried to ignore Teller's plan, and he hoped against hope that it was not a prediction. Being in the driver's seat gave him reassurance, but he knew that it was temporary, that he would have to act soon if they were to have any hope of escape.

Up ahead he saw a mound in the desert, and he knew the time to act was now. Instead of swerving to avoid it, he drove straight for it. He glanced back at Whistler, using that same silent sign language of the eyes. *Hold on tight.*

He turned sharply as they went over the bump, and the vehicle tilted to the right and tumbled over, hurling everyone who was not belted in. The vehicle rolled over several times, and Jacob struggled to hold on to his seat as bodies flung into him, as supplies bashed against him.

When the vehicle finally stopped its somersault, leaving their minds to continue where it left off, there was the briefest of moments where everyone was too dazed to think, and some were too dead to act. Light flooded in from the unhinged door, blinding the survivors. Then the previous commotion was replaced with a new one as Jacob scrambled for Teller's holstered weapon, and Teller grabbed his wrists, and a surviving soldier scrambled up and reached his arm around Jacob's neck. They shimmied across the broken glass, stumbling over bodies, bashing into the buckled sides of the carrier, pushing and pulling, tossing and tugging, fighting for every inch of this little battlefield, and every ounce of breath left in them. Jacob and Teller struggled for the trigger of the gun, and they struggled to point it just a few centimetres more towards one another, but it lingered there in the buffer zone between life and death.

Jacob heard a gunshot, and he knew that his finger did not pull the trigger. He tried to look down, to see if he had been shot, but the cry of the soldier behind him, and the loosening of the man's arm around Jacob's neck showed that he had been hit instead. Jacob gulped fresh breath, and his battle for the gun renewed.

Even as they struggled, Jacob could see Whistler waking up. His face now had blood to accompany the bruises. Jacob hoped he had not killed him before the Regime had a chance to. The boy was still bound, but the tumble had loosened some of them, and Whistler wormed his way out of the ones binding his wrists, and ripped the tape from his mouth with a cry. He did not try to untie his feet, but instead threw himself at Teller and tried to scrape and claw at him.

The three of them fell to the ground, scrambling for the gun, and it was a war of limbs, flying in all directions like a flail. In the flurry, Whistler might have been attacking Jacob as much as Teller, for they rolled about inside the remains of the carrier, bashing and striking, kicking and clawing. Here and there the gun fired into the ceiling or the walls, letting little blades of light in to illuminate their frantic battle.

Teller elbowed Whistler in the stomach, and the boy recoiled, coughing and clutching his aching abdomen. Jacob tried to grasp the gun, but Teller grabbed it first. Jacob tried with every ounce of strength to seize it off him, but it was all over. He heard the click of the trigger.

And nothing happened.

Teller growled as he realised there were no bullets left, but this only fuelled his wrath. He bashed Jacob with the gun, and Jacob desperately tried to shield his face. Blow after blow rained down upon him, and he felt his struggle waning, his resolve weakening. He could barely see through his swollen eyes, which were filled with tears and blood, and the blurry image of Teller's madness, of Teller's endless assault.

Then he felt the blows no longer, and he saw Teller cast the gun aside and stretch towards the boots of one of the dead soldiers. He pulled a knife from one of these, and he held it before Jacob's face, as if he wanted him to see the tool of his destruction. Jacob could see Teller's maddened eyes, magnified by his cracked glasses.

Then Teller prepared to lunge.

"No, please, no!" Whistler pleaded.

Teller paused, turning to Whistler, but keeping the knife close to Jacob's throat. Teller did not say anything, but the knife counted down the seconds to Jacob's death. He could almost hear the whispers of the blade.

"I'll tell you," Whistler said, forcing the words out through his tears. "I'll tell you where Dustdelving is."

"No!" Jacob cried out, feeling the knife almost slay the word.

"Tell me and I'll let him live," Teller said, and his voice was sickeningly sweet.

Whistler sobbed and looked to the ground, as if for answers. The dead who lay there provided none.

"Don't tell him," Jacob coughed, and Teller dug the knife in more, until Jacob was certain that any speech would slit his throat.

Whistler could barely get the words out, as if there was a knife to his throat as well. "I … it's … please don't—"

"Tell me!" Teller growled, and the fierceness of his voice would have almost made Jacob buckle and reveal the location.

"It's not here," Whistler bawled. "It's in the far … far south-west."

No! Jacob cried in his mind. He felt he could not cry it aloud. He knew that even if he could, it would not matter.

"Tell me the exact route," Teller said. "I will let him live if you tell me the exact route."

Whistler looked from side to side, and down, but never up, never at either of them, where he could see the reflection of his shame. His brow was forever furrowed, and it seemed as though he was fighting his own tongue, a battle of compassion and conscience. He rocked his head back and forth, as if he was trying to comfort himself.

"Tell me or he dies," Teller hissed.

"It's … you take … you take a right at—"

But Whistler's words were interrupted by a grunt from Teller, followed by a series of whistling sounds in the wind. Teller let go of Jacob and stumbled away, a dart lodged in his back, while a hail of darts fell on the armoured carrier and surrounding area.

Jacob immediately got up and ran towards Whistler, whom he grabbed and dragged with him out of the carrier, throwing him down into the sand as another barrage of darts came hurtling their way. Jacob felt the sharp sting of one in his forearm as he tried to shield Whistler, and when they got up he heard Whistler cry out as one struck his ankle, forcing him to limp and stumble away.

They ran for cover, but the only cover was behind them at the wreckage of the armoured carrier, which was being bombarded with a thousand darts. Teller hid there, searching for a weapon, and Jacob and Whistler fled south, until the darts pursued them no more.

"We will find you!" Teller shouted after them, and for the first time in Jacob's life he felt that it was true. He could not lay low in Blackout. Perhaps not anywhere in Altadas. As for Rommond's headquarters, it was a delving the Regime would make every effort to turn to dust.

Chapter Twenty-one

RUIN

Jacob and Whistler struggled south, Jacob supporting Whistler's arm around his shoulder. The boy limped, and Jacob bit back the growing pain in his wounded arm. Several times they collapsed in the sand, watched only by the unsympathetic sun, and Jacob began to worry that the darts were poisoned.

"I don't think we're going to make it," Whistler said, his breathing laboured.

"Don't say that," Jacob replied. He did not want to hear those awful, auguring words. "We'll make it," he promised to Whistler. *We'll make it*, he promised to himself.

He felt Whistler's curious eyes on him, squinting in the sunlight. "Thanks for saving me back there," he said.

"Thanks for saving *me*," Jacob replied. He caught a glimmer of a smile on Whistler's face, crushed by a grimace as he hopped along.

"Any time," Whistler said, but it did not seem like for either one of them there was much time left. Jacob could already feel the poison slither through his veins.

"Let's hope we won't need saving again," Jacob

said. If he had believed in a god, this might have been a prayer.

"Are we going in the right direction?" Whistler asked.

"Yes," Jacob said, though he really was not sure where they were going. All he knew was that they fled away from Teller and the nearby tribes. But perhaps they might have been going further into their territory. Jacob waited for the prick of another dart, another push closer to death. He had to shake his head to focus. His mind was becoming foggy.

"We need to get back to warn Rommond," he said.

"Don't tell them I blabbed," Whistler pleaded.

"I won't."

"But they'll guess."

"How will they guess?"

"'Cause I'm the only one of us two who knows the way."

"I think he'll understand."

"But what if he doesn't?"

"Look, kid, you did and said what you had to. Rommond will know that."

"If anything happens, it'll be my fault."

"No. If the Regime attacks the Resistance base, it will be the Regime's fault, not yours."

Whistler did not reply, but something told Jacob that the boy would still blame himself if Rommond's headquarters came under fire. If it was destroyed, there was no telling what he would do.

They continued across the seemingly endless sands, watering every grain with their sweat, anointing every granule with their strain. In the hourglass of time the sands continued to shift, and they could not find their way outside the glass. Their shadows struggled with them, hauling and heaving, dropping with them, and clambering up with them, and reminding them constantly that otherwise they were alone.

Then perhaps the hourglass turned, for they felt everything blur, and the world was tumbling. The red sand became black grains. Everything faded away.

Jacob awoke inside the Order's warwagon, with Taberah standing over him, and though her eyes were stern, they were also reassuring.

"We must stop meeting like this," Jacob said, and he noticed the weakness of his words.

Taberah did not smile. "You are lucky we meet at all."

"I think I got a little lost. Funny thing about sand—"

"You were poisoned," Taberah explained. "Our doctor was able to extract the poison."

"Looks like those tribes don't care who they shoot at."

"They care," Taberah said. "They just don't like us either."

Jacob sat up, wincing as he did. "Taberah, we need to discuss something important." The memory of Teller came back like a headache.

"Brogan already told me," she said.

"Everything?" Jacob asked.

"Everything."

"So what are we going to do?"

"We're going to evacuate the Order headquarters first. Teller knew exactly where that was. We are lucky that he was trying to find the way to Dustdelving or we might have been attacked earlier. That luck has now been spent."

The journey to the Order's headquarters was a sombre one, less like a journey home and more like a funeral procession. Few discussions were had, and those that did speak, spoke of evil things, and though they had not yet abandoned their home, they spoke like refugees.

Jacob was tended to by a nurse, perhaps the same nurse that had tended to him after the escape from the Hold. Whistler was in another room, nursing his own bruises, and Taberah came down the corridor several times to look in on both of them. Jacob feigned a smile each time she did, but she only had a frown to greet him, and she did not fake it.

As the night waned, Jacob found his restlessness did not wane with it. He tossed and turned, and eventually he sat up and stared out at the darkness, and listened to the tossing and turning of others around him. It seemed that few could sleep that night.

In time Jacob heard a knock upon his door, a soft knock, like that of someone not wishing to disturb those sleeping, or someone who had no great store of strength.

"Come in," Jacob grumbled. *It's not like I'm sleeping anyway.*

Whistler entered, still limping. His face brimmed

with bruises, disguising his usually pallid complexion. He gave a sheepish smile and waved his hand meekly.

"I hope I'm not disturbing you," he said.

"No," Jacob replied. "I couldn't sleep."

"Me neither."

"I can see that."

Whistler continued to stand by the door, as if he had not been invited to enter, as if there was some comfort beneath the safety of that wooden frame.

"Sit down," Jacob said. "You can forget your pleasantries with me."

Whistler sauntered into the room and sat at the end of the bed.

"We've been through a lot," Jacob said.

Whistler chuckled. "You could say that."

"Taberah said you told her everything."

Whistler hung his head. "Yes," he mumbled.

"How did she react?"

Whistler looked at the wall, where the shadows leaned in to listen. "She wasn't happy," he muttered. "She was very angry."

"I hope she realised that it wasn't your fault."

"I don't know," Whistler said despondently. "I told you I blab too much. She said I need a gag."

"That's not very nice."

"No. But maybe it's true."

"Look, kid, you're doing the best you can. That's all any of us can do. You shouldn't even be working for the Order. You're supposed to be out having fun. Haven't you got any friends?"

Whistler shook his head.

"Well, kid, I know what that feels like." He did.

Work as a smuggler earned him lots of contacts, lots of clients, lots of enemies even, but very few friends.

"So what do you do about it?" Whistler asked.

"I guess I need to make some new ones." He smiled and extended his hand to Whistler. "My name's Spider."

Whistler beamed and shook his hand. "Whistler here."

When morning came, the sun did not rise, and many considered it an ill omen, as if the Regime had blotted it out as a warning to the Resistance. *If there is no Hope for us, there shall be none for you.* People went about their business out of habit, routine crushing the depression that might have otherwise crushed them all.

They arrived at the Order headquarters at noon, according to the warwagon's chronometers, though the sky provided no confirmation of the time. The building looked somewhat grimmer under those clouds than it had before. Jacob almost wished for the uncompromising sun.

Though Whistler was still nursing many wounds, he jumped out of the warwagon before it came fully to a halt. Jacob tried to hold him back, but Whistler wormed his way from his grip and charged into the building, as if he had not been home in years.

"Let him go," Taberah said. "He always likes to go in first."

So Whistler went in first, and they could hear the patter of his feet and the panting of his breath as he passed from view behind the great metal doors.

They approached the doors of the Order headquarters slowly. Time always seemed to stop when in good company, as if time itself liked to forget its watch and join the party. Maybe the other Order members did not notice it, but it seemed like everything was different somehow.

They were almost at the door when Jacob saw a glint from the corner of his eye. Part of him thought to duck for cover, that it might be a glimmer of light reflecting off a gun. But he looked at the ground to his left and saw a single gold coil sitting there, waiting for him to pick it up.

"Just leave it," Taberah said.

"It could be lucky," Jacob replied. He felt compelled to take it.

As he approached it and reached out to it, he felt an odd sensation, like a tiny tremor in the ground beneath him. It made him pause, and everyone else paused as he bent down to take up this lonely coil. He almost thought he was rescuing it, placing it in the refuge of his wallet. Just when he heard it clink off the few other coils he had rescued previously, he felt the tremor grow suddenly in intensity. He turned around, just enough to see Taberah's worried eyes, and though time seemed to slow, it was not slow enough.

There was an immense and blinding explosion, which tore apart the Order headquarters, throwing Jacob and the others several metres in all directions. He tried to shield his head and face from the debris, but he felt a sharp sting as bits of metal and glass flew by.

He looked up at the burning wreck that used to be Taberah's home. From the corners of his eyes he could see people rolling about in agony. Had they gone inside, had they not delayed on the doorstep, they would be dead. He did not want to think of what had become of those that were still inside—like Whistler.

"Brogan!" Taberah cried, and she ran into the blaze before anyone could stop her. Jacob struggled up and charged after her, even though the flames tried to hold him back.

They scoured the building for the boy, searching every room, looking under every fallen beam, inside every nook that he might have hidden in. They found many bodies, charred beyond recognition, and a few of them looked about the size and stature of Whistler, but Jacob bit his lip and stepped over those remains, urging the survivors to keep looking, reassuring Taberah that he was there, that he must be there, that he must be still alive.

As Jacob wandered down corridors that seemed like the evil reflection of the ruined corridors of the Hope factory, he began to wonder if Rommond's worry was justified, if this was the Regime's swift revenge. He began to wonder if maybe Rommond was exploring the ruins of his own headquarters, or if he was exploring the afterlife instead.

In time Jacob found himself in his old room. Perhaps it was arrogant of him to call it that. It was just a place to stay, somewhere to sleep the night as he fulfilled an errand, as he completed a job that kept turning into something more. He was glad he was not asleep in it that day.

Most of the room was black, and it was hard to even be certain that it was his quarters, except for the large crate that stood prominently in the room. It was charred, but otherwise undamaged, a sole survivor in the carnage around. He opened the lid to see the lots of tiny survivors inside, glittering in glee at their good fortune.

"So much for the evacuation," he said.

Chapter Twenty-two

ANOTHER KIND OF HOPE

Jacob found Taberah in what he presumed was Whistler's room, slumped over a body. Every charred room looked the same, and every blackened body did also. She held the head close to her, as if to shield it from any further blows.

Jacob's heart sank, and he felt he had to leave the room, to escape this new prison of emotion that seemed somehow worse than his time in the Hold. Yet he could not leave, could not desert the woman who knelt with her child in her arms, and yet knelt alone.

Moments passed like the lives of the dead. Who knew how many had died in that explosion. The Order would not stay long enough to count. Names would be ticked off from a list later on, and their passing would not seem quite so bad on the page. Yet as people fell, the counters rose, and the anger rose in those who remained.

Then Jacob heard the sound of hope: a voice.

"Mother," it said, though it barely spoke at all.

"I'm here," Taberah said, though she mostly fought her tears.

"Am I going to die, mother?" Whistler asked.

He blinked through the soot and grime, through the cinders and the embers. Perhaps he even blinked through the pain.

Taberah struggled to respond. She muttered something, but Jacob could not make it out. Perhaps it was spoken in the tongue of the dead.

Jacob found all of this too much, and the urge to flee grew inside him again. He made for the door, but then he heard Whistler's voice call after him.

"Jacob," he said, another struggle, another strain. "Am I going to die?"

There was no escaping the question, just as there was no escaping death.

"No," Jacob replied as he stopped and turned around.

Whistler simpered.

They did not stay long in the ruins of the Order headquarters. Soasa urged them to return to the warwagon, bringing anything of value that they could find. Jacob made sure to haul his crate of coils aboard, while Taberah only hauled Whistler inside.

They sped off southward, fleeing their home-turned-Hell, and hoping against all hope that their destination would not turn out to be another place of fire and brimstone, a refuge only for devils. It seemed to many that they could not get there quick enough, that the desert had grown larger just to torture them.

Whistler's burns were treated by Doctor Mudro, who spent more time administering painkillers than anything else. When he tried to leave for a break, Taberah ushered him back inside, until Whistler no longer felt anything at all.

Jacob visited Whistler that night. Neither of them could sleep.

"You're not very lucky, are you?" Jacob commented.

"I'm still alive," Whistler said, forcing a smile. "You didn't lie."

"No," Jacob said. "No, I didn't."

"They gave me some leaf," Whistler said, and he slurred his words. "It makes me feel funny. I'm not sure what I'm thinking or saying. Maybe I shouldn't keep speaking at all. I keep getting us all into trouble. I don't mean it. Honestly, I don't. Maybe it ... maybe it would be better if when I go to sleep tonight I don't wake up."

"Don't say that," Jacob said. "That's the only thing I don't want to hear you say. You're being too hard on yourself. Look at all the trouble I get into. It's all part of the adventure."

Whistler smiled again. Perhaps that was what he needed. Adventure, not a war. Perhaps that is what they all needed. The Great Iron War was in its fifteenth year. The death toll no longer registered on Death's exhaustive lists.

"Jacob," Whistler said. "Am I a monster?"

"What? No, of course not."

"I mean," Whistler explained, "the scars. Do I look like a monster?"

Jacob paused to look at the bandages covering Whistler's face and body. The boy clearly could not see or feel them, and it was hard to tell just how bad the burns were underneath, or how bad the scars would ultimately become.

Monster was such a subjective word. It was what they called the demons that made up the Regime. Perhaps it was what the demons called them. Yet they all looked alike, so perhaps neither of them were monsters—or perhaps both sides were.

"You look fine," Jacob lied. "Better than me, at least. I think I could do with some of that leaf."

Whistler giggled, choking and coughing halfway through. He started to mumble something, and his eyes blinked erratically, and finally it seemed that he faded into sleep. Jacob hoped that he was luckier in slumber than the waking world. He also hoped, as he got up to leave, that in the boy's dreams there were no monsters.

As Jacob left Whistler's room he encountered Doctor Mudro, who was passionately puffing on the same leaf he had given the boy. It did not instil confidence in his treatments.

"How is he doing?" Jacob asked. "Will he recover?"

"Oh yes," the doctor said. "I've done my magic." He reached towards Jacob's left ear and produced a coil, which he rolled between his fingers.

"I wish I could do that," Jacob said. "All I find back there is dirt."

"Who knows what you'll find," the doctor said, producing an egg this time.

"I hope you did those tricks for Whistler."

"I've done better," the doctor replied.

"Will he have scars?"

Mudro paused. "Most likely. It's hard to tell at this stage. But yes. Most likely."

"Maybe your magic isn't all it's cracked up to be then," Jacob said.

The next day Whistler did not seem so bad. He sat up in his bed, and he stared out the window, and later that evening he wandered out of his room alone. His face and arms were still firmly wrapped with bandages, which he was sternly forbidden to remove. Jacob could see in Whistler's eyes that he did not need any such warning; he was afraid to remove them.

As night returned, and as the winding way to Dustdelving began to get the better of Jacob's stomach, Taberah asked him to see her privately in her quarters, which seemed a little sparser than they did before. He was glad of the distraction from Whistler and the journey. Perhaps she was too.

"I've heard word from Rommond," Taberah said. "He's ordering an evacuation. He expects the Regime to come after us, to hit back hard, especially now that they have a decent idea where Dustdelving is. We can't risk them destroying everything we've worked so hard to build up."

"I'm sorry about that," Jacob said.

"Don't be," she replied. "It isn't your fault."

He hoped she did not blame Whistler too harshly.

"So, what did you want to talk about?" he asked.

"Sit," she said, and she patted the bed beside her. Though it was the same gesture as that first night together, when her fiery locks ran down her shoulders, it was very different this time. She did not seem so inviting, and her hair was firmly tied up, as perhaps was her heart.

He sat down beside her, resting one knee upon the bed. He wondered how many men had wanted to sit in those chambers, how many men had wanted to be this close to her. He could still smell her perfume, though it was weaker than it was before, as if she no longer cared for such extravagances.

"Jacob, now that this is over—"

"I wish it was over," Jacob said. "Whistler said my nickname should be *Spider*, but why is it that I feel like I've been caught in your web?"

Taberah studied him for a moment as he studied her back. Perhaps she was wondering just what to do with this fly she had caught.

"Do you remember the night after we first met?" she asked.

Jacob grinned. "I sure do."

Taberah was not smiling. It was disconcerting.

"What if I told you that the amulet didn't work?"

Jacob raised an eyebrow. "I don't understand. You make them. Of course they work."

"In general, yes."

"What are you getting at?"

"I'm pregnant, Jacob."

Jacob shook his head. "I'm sorry," he said, as if he had heard the news of a departed friend. He had heard those lines before. So many women's lives ruined as they gave birth to demon children. So many more soldiers created for the Regime.

"I don't think you understand," Taberah said.

"I get it," Jacob said. "I'm not sure what I can say

to make it better."

"Then just listen, please."

Jacob crossed his legs and leaned forward, and he put on what he thought was his most comforting face. He hoped he did not come across as condescending.

"I'm one of the Pure," Taberah revealed. "It's not a myth. We're few, but we're real. I can give birth to human children. It's not a demon child, Jacob. It's yours."

Jacob faltered in his seat. He leaned back and uncrossed his legs. It was her turn to put on a comforting face, but it mattered little when coupled with those discomfiting words.

"Did the amulet not work?" was all he could think to ask.

"No," she said, and she looked as though she was going to add something else, but she held it back.

"You must be making this up," Jacob said. He could not conceive of the idea of the Pure being real, but then fifteen years ago he could not conceive of the idea of a demon invasion, and the Great Iron War that would be waged ever since.

"I assure you, Jacob, I am not."

Jacob took another deep breath. "I need some time to think about this."

"Of course. Take as long as you need."

"Eighteen years?"

"Not that long. He or she won't be a child any more."

"Exactly," Jacob said.

Taberah did not smile. "Maybe I don't want to joke about this."

"Sure," Jacob said. "But I still need some time to think."

Jacob had plenty of time to think as he helped with the evacuation of Dustdelving, but he found that he spent much of that wealth of time focusing on the duties at hand, and ignoring any other potential duties he might have to perform in nine months' time.

Rommond unveiled the means by which they would make their escape: a monumental submarine, adorned and embellished just like the Hopebreaker, and a vehicle that was as equally untested. In forcing Rommond's hand, it seemed he had to play all his cards.

They boarded the submarine swiftly, carrying on anything they deemed important. Jacob hauled his crate of coils to the loading bay, but he was stopped at the ramp by Rommond.

"What's that?" the general asked.

"My money."

"I said *bring the essentials.*"

"And I complied."

"Do you think the fishes will accept some coils?"

"They might," Jacob said with a grin. "I know I would if I were them."

"We can't afford the weight," Rommond stated. "Leave this behind."

"Are you mad? You're letting people bring all sorts of junk on board."

"Useful stuff, not junk."

Jacob shook his head. "Tell me in all seriousness that money isn't useful."

"If it's yours, then it's not useful to me."

"I'm the one who got you those nine crates in the first place! You wouldn't have your precious funding if it wasn't for me."

"Consider your safe passage through the deeps as payment for that service."

"I'm not coming without this."

"Then that is two weights we no longer need to worry about." Rommond walked off before Jacob could reply, leaving his only response the echo of him slamming the crate down upon the ground. The general ignored him, but many others looked his way.

"Is this what I get for helping you?" he shouted, aiming the words at everyone in the room, like a bomb that would strike all ears, even if it did not hit every heart. Those who were not already staring at him with worried expressions were doing so now. "I didn't have to, you know."

Rommond watched him coolly from across the room, where he consulted with his commanders, who looked as though they were dismissing Jacob as a madman. *Let them judge*, Jacob thought. *Let them sneer.*

Then Whistler hobbled up to him and grabbed his arm. His face was still cowled in bandages, his arms still wrapped tightly, and his eyes still showed the signs of the pain-numbing leaf. His grasp on Jacob's arm was very weak, and Jacob found him hard to look upon, and harder to think about.

"What are you doing?" the boy asked faintly.

"Making a scene," Jacob said. He bit back his frustrations, but they swarmed inside him, and he found it hard to curb his tongue.

"Rommond won't like that," Whistler told him.

"All the better."

"I don't like it," Whistler said.

Jacob did not have a response for that.

There were tears in Whistler's dazed eyes. "Rommond won't let you come if you act like this."

"Then I guess I'm staying behind," Jacob said.

"You can't. You'll be killed."

"Look, kid, I don't get to decide these things."

"Leave the money behind."

"I already refused fifty thousand coils for you," Jacob said. "I can't leave these behind."

"Why not?"

"I don't expect you to understand, Whistler," and he clasped his hands together firmly, as if praying to some silent god. "I *need* this. I *need* to bring it with me." He felt the spit spray from his clenched teeth, and he felt the veins protruding from his neck, as if every part of him was trying to reach out for that reassuring crate of coils.

The tears multiplied in Whistler's eyes, but Jacob knew that there were also tears in his own. He was glad the boy's tears did not reflect the manic look in his own eyes, but he had seen it in many mirrors before, and now it reflected from his memories.

Whistler ran out of the cargo bay. *Good*, Jacob admonished himself. *You've scared him.* He struggled to hold back another thought: *You scared yourself.*

Jacob sat on his treasured box for over half an hour before anyone approached him, and though he did not look up, he could feel the frequent stares of the passers-by. He glanced up only when he heard Taberah's voice.

"I've convinced Rommond to let you bring your spoils," Taberah said, and she sounded a little cooler than before. For a woman of heat, even the slightest drop in temperature felt like ice.

"Thank you," Jacob said.

"It wasn't easy."

Jacob cast a dirty look at Rommond. "I can imagine."

"Don't make it harder."

"Sorry," Jacob said. "Maybe I should say sorry to Whistler too."

"Would you still have wanted this crate if I hadn't told you about the baby?"

Jacob sighed. "I don't know. Probably."

"I've carried a child before," Taberah said, and she looked around the room for Whistler. "They can be heavy, but never a burden." She tapped her foot against the side of the crate. "I can't say the same for this."

Jacob forced a smile. "It's not going to get any lighter. I better get this crate on board then."

"Jacob," Taberah called as he walked away. He stopped and turned. "I'm sorry it had to be this way. But don't blame the child."

"I don't," Jacob said, and he walked away.

He dragged the crate on board the submarine, where Ensign Argan led him to his quarters, and made absolutely no effort to help him lift the crate—probably, Jacob presumed, on the strict orders of Rommond. When he finally reached his room, he found it barely big enough to squash himself into, let alone the crate, and thought this might be Rommond's doing as well.

As Jacob made his way to the bridge, he passed by a lot of people hauling a lot of things, including many machines he had never seen before in his life. Of those that were familiar, there were lots of them: landships by the dozen, artillery by the hundreds, guns by the thousands. He had to hand it to the general—he had certainly gotten his money's worth.

It took a long time to find someone who was not too busy to show him the way to the bridge, and then a longer time to get there. The submarine was huge, which made his own tiny quarters seem that much smaller. A civilization could live on this thing. With the Regime after them, he thought that they might have to.

When he reached the bridge, he tried not to barge in, even though he felt almost compelled to do so. The room was huge, with many control panels on display, and even beds in the corners for the on-duty crew. *Now these are quarters*, he thought.

"So," Jacob said, stretching his arms as if he had just gotten out of his web. Something told him that there would be more webs to snare him on the voyage ahead. "Have you a got a name for this tin can?"

Rommond looked at Taberah and smiled. "Yes," he said. "The Lifemaker."

About the Author

Dean F. Wilson was born in Dublin, Ireland in 1987. He started writing at age 11, when he began his first (unpublished) novel, entitled *The Power Source*. He won a TAP Educational Award from Trinity College Dublin for an early draft of *The Call of Agon* (then called *Protos Mythos*) in 2001.

His epic fantasy trilogy, *The Children of Telm*, was released between 2013 and 2014.

Dean also works as a journalist, primarily in the field of technology. He has written for *TechEye*, *Thinq*, *V3*, *VR-Zone*, *ITProPortal*, *TechRadar Pro*, and *The Inquirer*.

www.deanfwilson.com